Death at the Range

Carly,
♡ you & kick
butt in school
Nikki

Nikki Haverstock

ISBN: 1517068568

ISBN-13: 978-1517068561

DEDICATION

To John Haverstock, my supportive husband

CONTENTS

ACKNOWLEDGMENTS

I want to thank Deanna Chase and Violet Vaughn who showed me that Rockstar authors were people like me (kinda like me, they're cooler.)

Without Chatzy and RomanceDivas, I still would not have a clue.

Special thanks to Zara Keane and Zoe York who helped me put all the information into action. I owe you both hugs and endless drinks.

To my supportive family, thank you for only being slightly shocked when I said I was going to write a book.

Thank you to the Archery community, without you I wouldn't have a setting or any villains. Especially, Teresa Johnson who is my archery partner-in-crime.

Thank you to my amazing cover artist and editing team, you are the ones that made the book shine.

When opportunity "nocks"…

When a competitive archer is murdered at the training facility where Di has just started working, she's thrust into the middle of an unofficial investigation before she can even settle into her new life. With her roommate Mary and a Great Dane named Moo, she begins to unravel the mystery around the death of the victim, but can they solve the case before they find themselves in the killer's sights?

A wholesome cozy murder for every sleuth in the family

"Funny, charming, and occasionally deadly." ~ NYT bestselling author Zoe York

"A humorous first-in-series cozy mystery featuring a darling dog, a sassy heroine, and an amusing cast of characters." — USA Today bestselling author Zara Keane

This is the first book in a brand-new series set at the fictional Westmound Center for Competitive Shooting Sports in rural Wyoming.

Target Practice Mysteries

CHAPTER ONE

The Wyoming wind tore through my sassy lady pantsuit as I pounded on the glassed-in entrance to the Westmound Center for Competitive Shooting Sports. Apparently, what was acceptable for a Southern California autumn didn't cut it here. It had been a rushed two weeks to arrive, and I was inappropriately dressed.

Finally, a girl turned a corner at the end of the hallway, and I frantically rapped on the glass until her head swung in my direction. With her large, innocent eyes and smooth porcelain skin, she looked thirteen years old.

She called out as she approached the door, "Are you Diana?"

I wrapped my arms around my middle to stave off the cold seeping into my bones and nodded back. "Yeah, but you can call me Di."

She bounced on the balls of her feet as she unlocked the door then startled me by wrapping me in a hug and squealing with an enthusiasm normally reserved for lovers reuniting after war.

Before I could even pat her back she disengaged. "I'm so excited you are here. I've been here for a month and I'm bored out of my mind. We're roommates—I mean, not roommates, because we aren't sharing a room, but, like apartment mates. It's not really an apartment, but the closest thing we have here. It's my first time living away from home, and it will be, like, *so* nice to not be alone in there. The rooms are identical, but I can trade if you want. Everyone else is in meetings, so I'm just supposed to show you to your office then leave. But I can show you the apartment later, and do you want to have lunch?"

"Uh, can I come in?" I asked. I wasn't sure where

to start. I had only said a few words so far, and my brain was even farther behind.

I followed her down the wide hallways of the center. She was much shorter than me and radiated energy. Her shiny black, straight hair was pulled back into a tight ponytail. It was so short that it stuck straight out behind her, giving the appearance of great speed. Fitting since she spoke in a fast, clipped tone with large, round vowels that gave me the impression of a faint Minnesota accent.

My brain snapped into place. "I'm really sorry, but what did you say your name was?"

She slowed her pace and turned to me with a giggle. "I didn't. I totally forgot. Mary Van Dyke, a good Dutch name. And before you ask, yes, I'm adopted from Korea but grew up in Minnesota. Everyone always asks."

I had no intention of asking, though I had been curious.

She stopped in front of a door. "And here's your office. I've heard that you're going to be our new computer expert. You're pretty good with them?"

I ran a large tech company in Southern California; you could say I was pretty good. A few years ago, I would have explained my credentials in depth, but in recent months I've discovered that too much information led to questions I didn't want to answer. "Yeah, I'm pretty good. So what do you do around here?"

Her eyes lit up. "A bunch of stuff! I run the front desk mostly right now, but once we start in with the center's programs, I will do a little of everything: coaching, coordinating, writing press releases, whatever they need. But thank goodness you are here so I can skip the computer stuff. Plus, I take a few courses at the state university. I assume you're an archer? Why haven't I seen you at any competitions?"

I had been expecting this question and had worked on a nonchalant answer. "Oh, I competed in college, then life got in the way. You know how it is. I'm so excited to be getting back into the industry. This is where I need to be." It was true. This job was a literal answer to my prayers. A new state, new job, new life. It was a bonus that it revolved around archery. I loved archery.

"I heard that you just got divorced. That sucks."

A bark of laughter escaped my lips; it felt good. It had been a long time since I laughed. "Ya, it does suck."

Mary seemed nice. Who was I to turn down an overture of friendship? "Thanks for the tour."

"Sorry that I can't show you the rest of the horseshoe—that's what we call the building. I have to get back to the front desk. We open soon. Make yourself at home, and if you need me just holler." Mary hopped out the door, turned to the left, and trotted down the hallway to the front desk.

The office had a lot of windows. Next to the door was a large window that looked over the wide hallway then to a bank of windows on the indoor archery range. It was the largest indoor archery range I had ever seen. Mary said it was about ninety meters by forty meters, almost the size of a football field, which meant archers could train for outdoor distances of seventy meters in winter. Thank goodness for archery. It was the only reason I knew metric distances.

Walking over to the window, I could barely see the front door to the left where Mary had disappeared. The clock said the center would be open in four minutes. If I craned my head the other way, the hall stretched out of sight. There were flat-screen TVs on various walls, playing video footage of archery tournaments. The wall to the left was solid, but to the right there was another large window that looked out into a short hallway that led to a pavilion. The whole building was a huge, two-story horseshoe.

The interior of the horseshoe had a courtyard with grass and tables. It was probably lovely in summer, but in the October sun, everything was various shades of brown. Pressing my head to the window opposite the door that looked out to the pavilion, I was able to see the mountain to the south. When I had done research on Wyoming, I pored over pictures of Yellowstone National Park to the north, Medicine Bow National Forest a little south, and rural cowboy communities around winding rivers all over the state. Driving on Interstate 80, I had been surrounded by wide expanses of empty land, but once I exited the freeway I had approached tree-covered mountains.

Across the pavilion was the other leg of the horseshoe building. I could see banks of windows and a few people moving about but, it was far enough away that nothing was distinct. Ranges on this side were for archery, but on the opposite side, pointing away from the building, were the gun ranges. The soft thumping barely audible through the window let me know that the ranges were hot.

Tucked in a corner of my office was an easy chair. Looking back toward the L-shaped desk with two metal and plastic chairs, the tour was complete. Nothing left to do but sit down. As I lowered myself into the chair I locked eyes with a brown-eyed, short-haired, fuzzy head with twin shark-finned ears cutting the air above. Then it was gone, only to reappear a second later in my doorway followed by the largest black-and-white dog I had ever seen. With his short coat, it was easy to see he was male. The ragged black patches all over his body reminded me of a dairy cow. His large block head could easily reach my waist if I was standing.

He walked over to my chair and sat in front of me. I was neither familiar with nor frightened of dogs, but I had never met a dog without human introduction. "Hey, big guy, you come here often?" Humor was usually the best way to break an awkward moment.

He heavily dropped his head on my lap then swiveled his eyes up to mine. When I scratched behind his pointy ears, he let out a moan of pleasure.

On his blue collar there was a dog-bone-shaped tag with some phone numbers but no name. Instead, it said, "Westmound Center Dog."

He was definitely in the right building, but he must

have wandered into the wrong room. I shoved his head off my lap to peek out into the hallway for his owner, but it stretched out empty before me.

Before I could explore further, I heard the sound of heavy claws dragging across fabric. The dog had crawled into the easy chair in the corner. Turning one way then the other, he scratched the seat, leaving light marks on the industrial fabric.

"No, no, buddy," I futilely implored. He stopped to stare at me before circling three times and flopping down. His rump folded over one rounded arm, and his head hung over the other. It hardly looked comfortable.

"Di," a voice yelled from the door. The vowel was dragged out and ended in a squeal. My college roommate and the person who got me the job was at the door.

"Jess." I ran to her and threw my arms around her. We hadn't seen each other in person in years. Her dark curly hair tickled my nose, and my eyes stung with unshed tears. It was easy to forget the past year when no one knew me, but seeing a friend with years of history made it hard to forget how my entire world had imploded.

As she stepped back, she caught my eye. "No, none

of that. Remember, 'a clean start' and all the mumbo jumbo you fed me when you accepted the job?"

Laughter bubbled up inside of me, and my vision cleared of tears. In anyone else it would have seemed brusque, but Jess and I had gone through so much that she knew it would cheer me up. Some people dealt with pain by going to therapy, processing their feelings, and moving on. I cracked jokes. Sometimes it upset people when I laughed instead of cried, but I'd rather someone think I was a little daft than pity me.

There was no tissue in the room, so I used the inside of my right sleeve to dab at the corner of my eyes while Jess walked over to the dog. "I must've got something in my eyes. Welcome to my office."

She scratched him under the chin. He twisted in the chair, flipping on his back so that his large chest arched in the air. As she scratched down his neck to his chest, he rolled his head back over the chair's arm; his jowls flipped open, revealing a huge, toothy grin. The rows of large white teeth would be intimidating if it weren't for the grunting noises of pleasure he was making in time to Jess's scratches. Suddenly he sneezed, sending a fine mist of spray into the air. The action was so abrupt, his butt slid off the seat and landed heavily on the floor. He flipped over and leapt to his feet then looked at us innocently.

Jess giggled. "I see you met Moo."

So that was the dog's name. "You two know each other? We haven't been formally introduced; he sort of moved in. Should I take him back to his owner?" I glanced at Jess. Did dogs normally just wander around the building?

Jess grabbed the chair in front of the desk while Moo crawled back into his chair to lick a perfectly clean paw, leaving a growing wet spot on the fabric underneath. I didn't think I'd be spending much time in that chair.

Jess dismissed my concerns with a wave of her hand. "Nah, he gets free run of the place. He's a rescue and has special permission from Westmound headquarters to stay onsite. Just keep Moo off the ranges—safety protocol and all. He belongs to Lumberjack on the other side of the horseshoe, but Moo hates gun-fire, so he hangs out over here once the ranges open."

I felt like I had missed something in her explanation. "Why does a shooting range have a lumberjack?"

"Oh, that is just a nickname he has gone by for years. That's all people call him anymore." Jess pulled her briefcase on her lap.

The absurdity of the situation fit my mood. "Of course, that totally makes sense. A dog who has a special in with the Westmounds and is owned by someone that goes by the name of Lumberjack. Why didn't I guess that on my own?"

Jess made noncommittal noises while digging through her briefcase. I opened my mouth to start again, but she cut me off.

"I need to head out in a few minutes, let me get give you a few tasks to start with." Jess slid a piece of paper from her briefcase over the desk to me.

I had barely glanced at the page before she started rattling off a list of projects she wanted to work on with me. She discussed blogs, instructional videos, and camps then kept going. She seemed to hop from topic to topic with no discernable logic. Jumping into action, I searched through the drawers of my desk, looking for a pen and paper, but all I found was a collection of junk in otherwise empty drawers: a dusty dog toy, fletching glue for arrows, a bag of spare nocks for the backs of arrows, an Allen wrench set, and a tissue with chewed gum that I threw in the trash can. She showed no signs of waiting, so I started digging through my purse.

The tight, high-pitched, intense tone of her voice transported me a decade back to college. Every semester, during finals, we would go through this same thing. Everyone has anxiety at those times, but she took it to a whole new level. She would start winding herself up, and before I knew it she would be in the midst of a full-blown panic attack.

I saw the telltale signs: wide eyes with way too much white showing all the way around the iris, and her knuckles white on the handle of her briefcase.

I waved my hand while I leaned over the desk to get her attention. "Hey, whoa, hey now."

Jess looked at me, and the panic eased from her eyes. The color slowly returned to her face. She took a couple of slow, deep breaths. She was definitely in better control of her anxiety than she was in college.

Jess gave me a tight smile, a line of lips pressed tight, then put her purse on the ground. She took a deep breath then mumbled, "Sorry about that," under her breath.

I pushed back my shoulders, smiled, and focused on radiating confident energy. "How about you write down everything you think of, and once I'm settled in, then we can put together a plan for tackling these things. I'm not going anywhere." It was a skill I had perfected when I worked with clients.

The last bits of tension drained from Jess's face, and she sat back in the chair with an almost silent chuckle. "I really want to prove myself here. I know that everyone thinks I only got the job because Robbie was hired to run the entire center, but I know I deserve it. I've worked so hard and want to prove that I'm as qualified as anyone." Her voice was getting louder and higher as she talked. She was ramping up again, but this time with an eager energy. Her tone was balanced between thrilled and scared. She wildly gestured with her hands to emphasize her points. Robbie was her husband and a world-class rifle shooter.

Staffing had been a challenge since everyone had to move to Wyoming for the job. Part of the pay was in the form of onsite housing and food, making it an additional complication. Jess was more than qualified for the job; she had graduate degrees, coaching certifications, and any number of successful students. "You'll be great." My words sloughed right off on her as she continued to fidget with her papers. There seemed to be more to the story than I was hearing. "Did something happen between when we talked a few days ago and now? You didn't seem this… stressed then."

She slumped in her seat while rubbing her forehead. "We got the state grant to start a community wellness program, and several oil companies are interested in sponsoring our elite athlete training programs. We just got the news this morning at the meetings."

Struggling to see how that was bad news, I scrunched up my lips before replying. "That sounds like a good thing, right?"

"Yes, of course, that's part of the reason the center was put in Wyoming. The state and community is thrilled to have us here and is really supportive. It is just… well…… everything I dreamed of all these years. All the programs I have planned. I get to do them, and what if I can't? If they don't?"

"That's your worry? You have money and get to do all the programs you dreamed about?" I chuckled. "Call the news, rally the troops. There's a catastrophe going on—we have too much money."

Jess snorted from behind her arm, so I continued, "I'm not going to play the Divorce Card very often, but when you called me last month about this job, I was all, 'Wah wah, it's too much work, and I can't possibly move, get a new job, and get divorced at the same time.' And do you remember what you said?"

Jess mumbled from behind her arm, so I leaned over the desk, lifted her arm off her face briefly, then raised my voice. "I can't hear you."

She threw her arm off her face to reveal a smirk. "I said that you were awesome, strong, blah blah blah and could do anything. I'd be here to help."

"Yes, that blah blah blah got me through some hard times. If I can pick up my crumbling life mid-divorce, then you can manage your 'too much money and opportunities' problem."

"Have you been talking to someone?"

I knew she was asking about the divorce. "No, I decided to handle it differently. I'm going to ignore it and pretend it isn't happening. That's why I'm paying a lawyer; it's her job to worry about things."

A tiny frown formed on Jess's face as she softened her voice. "Oh, Di, I really think—"

"I'm a WASP; it's the way of my people to bottle things up." Jess stared at me while I fought against the urge to fill the air with explanations. The moment stretched out painfully until I felt like it would snap back at me. I attempted to break the moment by changing topics. "What the heck am I supposed to do here?"

Jess straightened in her seat with a startled exclamation. "I almost forgot. Next Monday you will join the department head meeting. Everyone is excited to meet you. They are off putting together projects to use you. That's why I had to rush over and remind you of your allegiance to me."

She gave me a dramatic wink before continuing.

"Here is your basic meeting schedule. The first is with the outside tech company we are using; they should be able to get you whatever it is you need. The rest of the meetings are with various center employees so they can let you know what their department needs. You are going to have a lot of down time, so feel free to spend the rest moving into employee housing, buying what you need, and if there is any time left over, you can start learning about the sports represented here. The bottom of the schedule has a half dozen links. That will keep you busy until we start coach training at the end of the week."

I looked at the sheet. Everything seemed pretty clear cut.

Jess started to rise, but I had one more question. "What about Moo?"

At the mention of his name, he looked up at me and yawned. His mouth was wide enough to eat a whole loaf of bread in one bite, and his tongue flopped out. I patted my thigh, and he crawled out of the chair and walked over to me. He stood next to my chair and abruptly shifted all of his weight to my side, causing the chair to slam into the desk. I braced my feet on the ground and gave his rump a good scratch. "Do I need to let him out or anything?"

Jess looked at the now vacated chair with its drool spots and copious dog hair and lifted her upper lip in disgust. "Nah, just don't lock him in here, and he'll be fine. He has a doggy door to an enclosed run on the far side of the building. He's our easiest employee."

She gave me one last hug and left me to get settled into my first new job in eight years.

CHAPTER TWO

The week flew by as I settled into a new pattern and life. Mary had been thrilled to escort me to the nearest mall to pick up athletic clothes that met the dress code of the center and Wyoming winter jackets and shoes. A quick trip to the pet store while in town had ended in a dog bed, snacks, a water bowl, and a few toys. Moo didn't belong to me, but he seemed to think it was his duty to spread dog hair over every inch of my office. The chair he had claimed as his own was discolored from his drool and starting to creak when he crawled into it. I encouraged him to stay off it before it collapsed and instead use his new dog bed (in the shape of a heart, because it came with an adorable doggie toy and matching blanket for only three dollars more). More often than not he sprawled across the bed with most of his body off the bed or all four feet in the air as he squirmed across the surface. I still hadn't met his owner but I had come to think of Moo as mine—a warm, calming creature to share my work-day with. He felt like an ally while I met the various department heads.

I kept the center's personnel webpage open throughout the meetings so I could start to learn the staff's names. I had met almost everyone there except for the most interesting one, Liam Andersson. Unlike the rest of the pictures, which consisted of headshots with a professional blue background, Liam's was an outside shot of him firing a gun. He leaned forward toward the target, a cloud of dust around his body while he squinted into the sun. His hair was clipped short on the side but longer on top, and he had a full beard. He looked like something out of a video game, or a Viking brought back to life.

His job description said "Equipment," which didn't make much sense as a job description. I hadn't spotted him in the halls or cafeteria, but I had mixed feelings about meeting him. The mystery of a hypothetical man was enticing since I was in no place to deal with a real man, at least not romantically.

Mary ran into my office, wiped a layer of dog hair

off the plastic seat, collapsed into the chair, then pulled it to my desk. "Oh my goodness, I have so much to tell you."

I didn't bother to hide my smile as I swiveled to turn to her. Last night she drove to Denver to pick up the Summer Games athletes who were arriving for the coaching course that started in twenty minutes. I went to sleep before she returned, and when I left this morning Mary was still sleeping.

"So much drama about the new coaches' course. The four Summer Games archers that flew in are not happy about being here, and there is all this tension between them. The drive back was so weird."

Mary loved to gossip, and I didn't complain. Whenever she wanted to ask about my life, a topic I did not want to discuss, I could distract her by asking about other people. "Tell me." I knew she didn't need much encouragement, and I was right, as she launched into her story.

"I picked the four of them up at the airport, and the girls, Minx, Owley, and Honey, are all sitting at least fifteen feet apart."

"Their names are ridiculous; at least Allie is a normal name."

"Not Allie. Owley, like an owl? Anyways, we get the luggage into the van, and Tiger hops into the first bench seat, and Minx crawls in next to him. Owley says she needs to sit there because she gets car sick, but Honey suggests that if Owley gets car sick, she should sit up front with me, not next to Tiger. They all just stand there snipping at each other about where everyone was going to sit. A cop had to come over and yell at us to move. Minx yelled at Owley and Honey to stop acting like babies and crawled into the front seat next to me. Owley got in next to Tiger, and Honey went into the row behind them."

I sucked air in through my teeth, surprised. This could make for a more exciting coaches' course. Drama can be fun to watch when you aren't part of it. "Yikes, are they always like that?"

"I have no idea." Mary burst into a huge smile. "I've never spent much time around them in private, just at tournaments. I had no idea they fought like this when they were alone."

Mary lightly bounced in her seat. She reminded me of the saying, if you don't have anything nice to say, then come sit by me. We had started to bond over our shared love of mocking reality stars on TV.

"Were there just the"—I stopped to count in my head—"four of them? Didn't we send six archers to the Summer Games?"

"Yes, only four of the six archers came to coach's training, and they were not happy about it. Minx complained it was stupid that after attending the Summer Games she had to come to a class to learn how to teach archery." Mary broke into a falsetto voice. "I can represent my country at the biggest archery event in the world, but I have to take a class to teach archery. What a bunch of horse… um, crap."

"Horse crap? Such harsh language! What did everyone else say?" I couldn't help teasing Mary about her obviously edited version of the story. Mary's sweet nature, all gossiping aside, had become evident over the past week.

Mary put her fists on her side and huffed at me. "You know what I meant. Owley just shrugged, but she doesn't say much ever. Honey said she was happy to attend the first course on the new coaching curriculum—or was it that she would be glad to be one of the first coaches of the new system? I can't remember what she said. It was all about Honey, Honey, Honey. I think she even used the phrase 'Master

Plan.' Can you believe it?"

I giggled. "Master plan? What is she, an evil villain?"

Mary looked at me with big, round eyes and got up. "Yes, she is."

I turned to Moo, who was lying on his back with his dog bed on top of him. He was chewing on a corner while scratching at it with his front paws. "Hey Moo, do you wanna go with me?" I got no further than "wanna" before he leaped up and pranced, his front paws dancing back and forth. He reacts that way to every question that starts with "Do you wanna," but still it made me feel like we were a team when he bounded into action.

I had placed a whole set of human emotions on his actions, but after losing my entire social group last year, it was a joy to have a creature that wanted to be with me. Looking at Mary waiting at the door, I had to admit that I had another friend in her.

I grabbed the driest corner I could find and held the dog bed out to my side to avoid getting even more dog hair on my pants, then the three of us headed into the hallway. There was only one more question left to answer.

"What did Tiger say?" I spoke in a whisper so my voice wouldn't carry.

"He said he was happy to be anywhere when he was surrounded by such pretty ladies, then he winked at me in the rearview mirror. He's so hot." Mary let out a deep sigh.

I turned to look at her, and Moo barreled into the back of my knees. I pitched forward, wind-milling my arms, and almost smacked Mary with the dog bed before catching my balance. "Good grief, have you got a crush on him? He sounds cheesy."

Mary's head snapped around to look at me. "No, I don't have a crush on him, but if I did, it would be totally justifiable. He's passionate, sweet, and one of the top-ranked archers in the world. Very talented. You will understand once you meet him." A big, goofy smile broke across her face. "Plus, he's so cute."

Mary had a crush on Tiger. I smiled to myself. "Who else is taking the class?"

I figured Mary had snuck a look at the participant list, and I was not disappointed.

"Jess is teaching, but you know that. Then the three of us are taking the class—you, me, and Bruce, who runs the community archery program here. The

Summer Athletes I picked up. The rest are various archery coaches from Wyoming and Colorado. The housing isn't finished yet, so only the Summer Athletes are staying here. Minx, Honey, and Owley all had a fit about who was going to stay where since someone would get their own place and the other two would share a room. In the end, they each got their own suite just to shut them up. It was 1:00 a.m., and I thought Robbie was going to bust a vein. He left early this morning with most of the center staff for Oregon."

We entered the room laughing, and I peeled off toward the back to reserve two seats and secure a spot for Moo's bed. Behind me, I heard a man approach Mary and ask about her mother. Mary must know everyone in the archery community.

I found a table at the far back with two chairs and two matching piles of paperwork. I threw down the dog bed so Moo could start the elaborate process of scratching, sniffing, and circling required before he sat down. I dreaded the meeting, and his snuffling and snorting was comforting. I was excited by the course in the hypothetical sense, but the actuality of being stuck in a seat for hours was something I resented.

Working at the center had been a dream so far

because they encouraged any activity in line with the vision of an 'athletic center.' As long as I kept my phone on me, I was allowed to go to the weight room or ranges at any time. The center's structure of metal and concrete blocked cell signal, but we had wireless throughout the building and a dedicated messaging system. The entire staff had keys to the building and weight room. We also had keys to ranges in our specialty. I had keys to the indoor archery ranges, and once I went through their safety training, I would get keys to the firearm ranges.

Looking around the room, it was disappointing to see so few women though I was used to it after working in the tech field. Three gals around my age or younger hung near the front but with large spaces between them. They seemed to be orbiting around a handsome man. He sat in a chair balanced on its back legs while he laughed. A few of the older men came over to shake his hand and greet the girls in turn. I pegged them as the four Summer Games archers holding court.

Off on the other side of the room was the rest of the group in a large circle, having an animated discussion. Among them was a single tall female, her arms crossed except when she gestured with a pointed finger at the man directly opposite her. I guessed they were the local coaches, as their body posture denoted them as peers.

Jess caught my eye and nodded but didn't move to come over to me. A small knot of anxiety was tightening in my chest. I had not even touched a bow in six years since I 'loaned' my equipment to the daughter of a couple from church. All I had left was my original finger tab. It protected your draw fingers from the string and was molded to my hand. I kept it in my desk drawer like a talisman of lost dreams. It was the first thing I packed when I left the company. Like a security blanket, I had kept it on my bedside table as I spent sleepless nights deciding what I was going to do with myself after I moved out of our home during the divorce.

I pulled it out of my pocket and laid it in front of me. The leather was worn smooth from shooting all through college. The cords attaching it to my middle finger had been replaced by a custom shoe string with stars on it, the metal at the top ground down to perfectly fit my hand, and the spacer that slid between my first and middle finger was shaved down. Everything about it was customized for me. How had I gone from an athlete to a lump that hadn't competed since college?

I slid it back into my pocket to end its judgy stare.

I was lost in my own thoughts. It took a minute for me to register that Jess had started talking. People moved around to find a seat, and Mary grabbed the chair next to me.

"…Center for Competitive Shooting Sports is dedicated to not only introducing the public to shooting sports in a safe and professional environment, but we are also passionate about assisting the elite athlete in their training. With this in mind, I'm honored to present these to our archers who have represented our country at the international level."

Jess pulled out four keys on keychains.

"These keys will open the center, weight room, and archery ranges at any time. Please consider the center your home away from home."

A smattering of applause started around the room as Jess beamed and handed out the keys. She handed the first key to the good-looking man, confirming that he was in fact Tiger.

"This wouldn't be the first time a pretty gal gave me a key." He turned to the coaches behind him, who gave a dirty laugh.

Rolling my eyes, I turned to Mary, who was

giggling.

Jess handed the next key to a gal next to Tiger. The woman had angled herself to be half facing Jess and half facing the classroom.

"Gee, thanks, Jess, super useful for all those times I'm in the middle-of-nowhere Wyoming."

Her tone was light and joking, but it was a rude thing to say in reply to a gift. A few people laughed, but I saw Jess's mouth briefly tighten before replying.

"You raise a great point, Minx. I think it is the perfect time to mention the fact that we are in the process of creating the official OSA program. OSA stands for On-Site Athlete program, which should be accepting applications by the new year. This program will allow elite and up-and-coming athletes to train at this state-of-the-art facility, with food and housing provided in exchange for a very light work schedule. Not only will they have unprecedented training, but their work schedule will be flexible to account for competitions."

A murmur of whispers filled the room as Jess handed out the other two keys. I had known about the announcement but didn't realize what an impact it would have. Jess reminded me of an infomercial salesman with her slow, deliberate delivery and over-the-top description, but it seemed to be working. Tiger and Minx exchanged a glance before Tiger got Jess's attention.

"Jess, you'll be sending me the application when it's available, right?"

"Absolutely. We hope all elite athletes will consider this opportunity, and coaches, please pass this on to students you think could benefit. We are looking for dedicated, passionate archers."

The blonde gal stood up to address the group with the mannerisms that seemed as though she was doing us a great favor.

"I want everyone to know Tiger and I might be busy with obligations. As Summer Games athletes, we have a duty to our fans."

Tiger blew out a heavy sigh. "The TV show isn't a given, Honey. Don't make it sound like such a big deal."

She turned to glare at him, her fists balled. "Don't say a thing, Tiger, we are not supposed to say anything until the contracts are signed."

He smirked at her, completely unaffected by her anger. She stomped her foot, and he started laughing.

"Who in the world would put you two on TV?"

Minx played with her keychain.

The whole room went silent, leaning forward to listen.

"Who wouldn't want to see archery's greatest power couple on TV?" Tiger leaned back in his chair.

Mary grabbed my arm, her tiny fingers digging into my flesh as she quickly whispered in my ear, "I knew there was something going on between them."

From up front, the last remaining Summer Game athlete, who must be Owley, spoke up.

"Couple?"

She looked at Tiger then Honey before turning back to Tiger. Her face was completely smooth, her jaw hanging open the tiniest bit. Her voice was higher than I expected but as absent of emotion as her face. The resemblance to an empty-headed owl was staggering.

Minx blew out a loud raspberry. "A couple of what? You two aren't dating." She hit the word dating extra hard, with implication I didn't understand.

Honey glared at her, biting off each word individually. "Don't be jealous, Minx."

Tiger looked at Minx with a raised eyebrow and blew her a kiss. Honey crossed her arms and pursed her lips at Tiger.

The coaches' heads swiveled as they followed the conversation like a tennis match. Mary was staring with rapt attention, like she was watching the screaming housewife show she loved.

Suddenly, Honey's whole face changed to a brilliant smile, and she turned to the class again. She put her hands out to hold us at bay, as though we were about to rush her in excitement. "And I have one more bit of news that I know everyone will be thrilled to hear. My personal memoir, covering my entire archery career since I started shooting in college through the Summer Games, will be available very soon. So many people have been begging me for years to share my inspirational story, and I finally found the time to write it all down. Don't worry, it's full of the juiciest gossip in the industry, and I'm sure you will recognize some names."

Pointedly, she looked at Owley, Minx, and Tiger in turn then shot a glance back to the class, but I couldn't see who exactly she looked at before she sat back in her seat.

Jess had been standing at the front watching, but with a shake of her head she finally spoke up to bring the conversation back to the coaches' course.

"Let's dig into the material. We will be doing a quick overview of the new level 1 and 2 course before lunch, then afterwards we will hit the range with beginner bows to go over the basic form steps and make sure we are all on the same page with the US Archery Form System."

***

After lunch, we headed over to the practice range. Mary and I jogged down the hallway to burn off the extra energy stored up from sitting all morning. I had a bundle of anxiety in my chest at the idea of shooting. I was looking forward to it in the way you look forward to seeing a best friend that you have lost touch with. Would it be the same? Could I still shoot? What if I hated it now? Why was I so nervous?

We had spent the morning going over the USAFS, US Archery Form System, which was the way all American coaches were being required to learn. The idea was a student could go to any coach and learn the same system. It was developed by the US National Coach for Archery. This was the first class with the new literature. Most of it covered the same things I had learned in college but with a specific name for each part of the shot cycle. The morning class had crept along as coaches asked for justification or wanted to share their view on why their way was better.

The worst offender was Honey. At least three times she stood up to say, "What I think Jess is trying to explain is…" I was ready to strangle her, but at least half of the class nodded along with her explanation. Every time Honey spoke up, Jess's mouth tightened into a thin line until she would wrestle back control of the class.

After the third time, Minx told Honey, "If you slow down this class any more, I'm going to stab you in the eye with my pen." After that, things moved a little faster.

Jess spoke loudly over the din on the range.

"Everyone grab a bow, a bow sling, and some arrows. We are using these beginner bows to make sure we know all the steps and to practice coaching each other. Please make sure you are using USAFS even if you use a different form yourself."

Mary was next to me, and we hung back as people paired off and grabbed equipment. They were guests and had first dibs.

Bruce, the director of community archer education at the center, made a bee-line for Owley and pulled her off to the side. Honey stepped in front of them and said something I couldn't hear. Bruce snapped back at Honey through bared teeth and stepped around her, dragging Owley out to the hallway.

As the crowd lessened, Mary and I stepped forward to pick up our equipment. Jess was getting all the pairs lined up in front of targets set at half the normal distance for inside shooting. Without the top-end equipment on the bows, like sights, clickers, and stabilizers, we would be happy to keep the arrows on the target mats.

Jess called out, "Hey, Honey, Tiger, would you be able to switch with Di and Mary? I think they could learn a lot from you two."

Honey looked between us and Tiger for a split second before a smile crossed her face.

"Yes, I would love to help out Mary." She beckoned Mary to come over. "I've been wanting to ask Mary something anyways, but first, how's your mom?"

Tiger jogged over to me. "I guess that means we are a match, eh?" He waggled his eyebrows at me. My glance shot over to Honey to see if she was watching. Tiger followed my glance then pursed his lips.

"Don't take all the power couple stuff too literally; it's for reality TV, more or less." He made finger quotes around the word reality.

Jess blew the whistle once, indicating it was clear to shoot, and I was lost in my own world. Even after all this time, my fingers remembered how to grab the arrow by the nock and snap it onto the string with one hand. My bow hand turned to move the elbow out of the way while my fingers in the finger tab were set into a deep hook on the string, the back of my hand smooth and flat, making a continuous line from the first knuckle to my elbow. Raising the bow, I drew back until I had a firm anchor, my draw hand pressed hard to my jaw-line, the string hitting the corner of my chin and the tip of my nose. My back held the weight at full draw and felt amazing.

Back in California, many of my friends raved about yoga, and while I enjoyed it, I never found the pure bliss they did in the movements, but now I understood. The movement, the tightening of muscles, the stretching—all of it felt right and where I should be. How could I have ever stopped shooting?

Tiger interrupted my thoughts. "You look great."

I turned to him and rolled my eyes at what I thought was flirting. He chuckled but clarified.

"That too, but seriously, your shooting form is

great. How long have you been shooting? Why aren't you competing?"

"Thank you. I used to compete in college, but that was years ago." I was embarrassed and pleased. He was kinder than I had expected after watching him in the classroom in the morning. I could see his appeal.

"Then you definitely need to get back to it; you're a natural." He smiled at me. I could feel a blush starting to form when Jess interrupted us.

"She's always had natural form. She should start shooting again, but right now you two need to focus on the exercise." She cocked her head at us and raised her eyebrows until we nodded. Tiger and I exchanged a quick smile then got back to work.

***

Rolling over in bed, I grabbed the phone off the side table to check the time. 1:00 a.m. The afternoon training had run right up until dinner time, when most of the class had left to go home or to a hotel. The rest of us grabbed dinner in the cafeteria. Since the archery side of the center was closed for the coaches' course, Robbie had gone with the firearms instructors to a camp in Oregon to see what comparable programs were doing.

Mary and I had gone to bed in our separate rooms in the unit we shared, but sleep had escaped me. All sorts of old emotions had been riled up and demanded attention. At dinner, Honey had announced that I hadn't changed at all, which was a surprise considering I had never met her before. Or so I thought. Turns out that before Honey was known as Honey, she was known as Joyce. Joyce had been a freshman who joined Jess's and my college archery team our junior year. Joyce wanted to be a Summer Games athlete and decided archery was the easiest sport to pick up. This had not made her very well liked on a team where everyone loved archery.

But I guess Joyce, or rather Honey, had been right since just a few months ago she had attended the Summer Games. What if I had kept competing? Honey had not been a natural archer, her form awkward and forced.

Every time I rolled over, I was plagued with what-ifs and unanswered questions. Maybe some running would help. Slipping on some workout clothing and a heavy jacket, I grabbed the center key and snuck out the door. The sky was crystal clear, and a blanket of stars stretched out endlessly over-head as I trotted to the

Firearms entrance. When the center was closed, the only way to get in, even with a key, was by unlocking the door on that side. I kicked off my heavy snow boots in the area between the front door and the second set of doors and slipped into the hallway, carrying my workout shoes. It was dimly lit at night, with the bank of dark rooms and offices on the side.

Passing the only open door, I glanced inside to see a room crowded with guns, bows, and tools on shelves and in cabinets. It was a large room, not entirely visible. Noises rolled out of the room, muffled and indistinct. But, much to my delight, I locked eyes with Moo. Between his large paws was a green stuffed animal. Bits of green fake fur clung to his lips and nose as he hopped up and trotted into the hallway to join me.

I gave him an ear scratch while I plucked a large ball of green fuzz from his lip. "Wanna keep me company in the weight room?"

He wagged his tail.

I debated telling whoever was in the room that Moo was joining me but didn't really feel like talking or explaining why I was wandering the halls with bed-head and no makeup in the middle of the night.

We walked down to the weight room. I propped

open the door and flipped on the lights. Moo pushed into the room ahead of me and jogged over to the black rubber flooring by a bank of free weights. Turning around, I startled hard at the realization someone was already in the room, laying on the floor. As I advanced, I recognized Honey's blond hair.

I called Moo back to my side and gripped his collar hard. Something was very wrong. Honey's shirt was disheveled, and one pant leg was pushed up to her knee. She was perfectly still, with eyes that stared straight ahead. Her head was tipped away slightly, the back of her head matted with blood.

CHAPTER THREE

"Help! Help!" a voice rang out, and after a second I realized it was my own. I grabbed the handle on a treadmill to steady myself. The sensation of my hand gripping the firm foam felt distant and hazy.

A noise behind caused me to spin around. A Viking stood in the doorway, scanning the room with piercing light eyes. He raced over to me, and I recognized him as Liam from the employee website.

"Help her! She was here. I-I just walked in. There. Not moving. She's... she's not okay." I ended in a sob, and the room shifted around me.

Liam grabbed my arm hard and dragged me outside the doorway into the hall.

"Sit. Head between your knees, push against my hand, and breathe in slowly on my count."

As I slid down the wall to put my head between my knees, he gently pushed on the back of my neck and counted slowly to five as I matched my ragged breath to his count.

"Good, now breathe out slowly."

I was still gripping Moo's collar tightly in my hand, and slowly I became more aware of my surroundings. Like a feather drifting down to earth, my mind settled more firmly in my body. My breath slowed as I looked into Liam's eyes.

He searched my face for a second. "You're looking a bit better. Are you okay if I leave you?"

I nodded and hugged Moo, and he laid his head on my shoulder. Liam headed into the weight room. Soon I heard his mumbled voice drift into the hallway. He must be using the center phone in the room. I couldn't catch his side of the conversation, although the tone of it carried into the hallway, deep and safe. I focused on my breathing, slow and controlled.

After a few seconds, or perhaps a lifetime, he came into the hallway.

"We are going to need to move to the entrance to let in the police. I gave them the code to the front gate, but we'll need to open the center door for them. They'll be here in a second."

He spoke carefully and slowly as though I was a child, but it seemed appropriate since I felt so out of sorts.

"Shouldn't…" I stared back at the door. "Shouldn't one of us stay with her?" The idea of her just lying there alone was too distressing.

He pulled me up and put my free hand through the nook of his arm to support me.

"She's not suffering. There's nothing we can do for her now, and we need to stay together."

We slowly walked through the empty hallways back to the entrance. Liam unlocked the large glass doors then sat down next to me, up against a wall. I let go of Moo, and he lay down next to me, pawing at my foot until I started petting him.

"Hey, are you feeling a bit better? You gave me a good scare."

I took a deep breath and let it out in a huff. "I'm feeling a bit better." I paused before sharing what was heavy on my mind. "It wasn't an accident, was it?"

He turned to look at me, though I kept my eyes on the wall ahead.

"Why do you say that?"

I gave a shrug. "I don't know. It just felt..." I couldn't put it into words. Something had been wrong, but I didn't know what. "I read a book that said your gut instinct in situations is very accurate, and I guess it just doesn't look like an accident. But I want to be wrong..." Poor Honey.

"I don't think you are wrong. There was nothing around her, but something had obviously hit her on the back of her head."

I sniffled. If it wasn't an accident, then someone had done it on purpose. "Who would have done that to Honey? It wasn't me, I just got here."

"I know. After Moo left, I poked my head out into the hallway to see who it was. He normally sticks right by me after the ranges close."

Moo lifted his head to stare at Liam when he said his name. Liam leaned forward to give him a little scratch. With a start, I realized that we hadn't even introduced ourselves.

"Moo sticks pretty close to me during the day. I'm Di." I awkwardly turned to offer my hand. "If Moo belongs to you, then you must be Lumberjack?"

He winced at the name. "No, call me Liam please."

"I'm sorry, I thought Jess said that Moo's owner

prefers to go by Lumberjack?" Had I remembered that incorrectly?

"Yes, some people call me Lumberjack, but really Liam is fine. It's this thing that everyone has for pro names." I stared at him, confused.

"Professional names," he clarified. "A few years ago, one of the top professional Compound archers decided to go by a nickname. He put it on shirts and what not. Then all the top archers decided they needed pro names. Suddenly everyone was Cheetah, Wolverine, or Honey Badger. I have a beard, wear plaid shirts from time to time and suddenly I was dubbed Lumberjack. If you stand still long enough, you get a nickname. I have fifteen-year-old kids that haven't even competed nationally writing me with sponsorship requests. They have their pro name all picked out. It is kinda ridiculous, it's not like we're…"

He had become more animated as he warmed up to the topic. He flapped his hands around as he searched for the right term.

I wiped at a tear and tentatively replied.

"A bunch of rappers?"

He smiled at me. "Yes, exactly."

It seemed like a long time ago that coaching

training started and I met everyone with a pro name, which reminded me. "Why are you here? Aren't all the gun people gone?"

"The instructors and directors are gone, but I don't really fall into that category. I deal with equipment for both sides of the horseshoe, guns and bows. I'm still getting the equipment room inventoried and set up. I really should have come by and met you sooner, but I have been working later and later each day."

I pulled my knees to my chest and rested my cheek on them, turning my head so I could watch his face. "Is that why you are here so late?"

"Yeah, I grabbed a snack from the kitchen as the cafeteria closed and headed to the equipment room and have been there ever since."

"And you didn't leave?"

"Nope, not even once."

I searched his face for deceit. "Not even to go to the bathroom?"

He chuckled. "Nope, the equipment room has an attached bathroom. It needs a sink area for cleaning gear so it made sense to just finish it out. Don't worry, Ms. Detective, you haven't been sitting with a killer."

Lights filled up the glass entrance as several cars

parked. We stood up to face the inevitable questions.

Liam pushed the doors open to welcome the officers but turned back in the doorway.

"Why don't you keep Moo with you tonight and make sure to have an officer escort you back to your room?"

I couldn't believe this was happening. Someone had killed Honey. I shivered and pulled Moo close.

CHAPTER FOUR

I was roused from sleep by Mary leaning over me and poking me in the shoulder.

"There are police everywhere. When did Moo get here? What's going on?"

I stared at her for a few seconds while I tried to get a handle on where I was and what was happening. My knees ached from the weight of Moo sleeping on them. The bed was small, and Moo took up a significant portion. I had laid out a blanket on the floor, but he had obviously decided that he could easily find a spot on me. His body warmth seeping through my brand-new flannel comforter and deep breathing had been a comfort that outweighed my contorted position.

Slowly, memories of the previous night filtered through my mind and brought a frown to my face.

"Mary," I gently said, "you need to sit down. I have to tell you something."

She grabbed a chair from the desk while I scooted up to lean against the wall so I could look her in the eyes while I talked.

"Last night, I couldn't sleep, so I got up and went over to the center to run. When I got to the weight room, Honey was there, uh…" I hesitated; I had never had to share this kind of news and was unsure of what to say. "Honey's dead." I ran through the rest of the story briefly as best I could. When I finished, Mary sat there briefly before responding.

"Poor Honey. I can't believe she was murdered." She got up to grab a few tissues from my small bathroom and handed one to me.

We dabbed at our eyes. "Yeah, Liam was pretty sure, and based on how the police questioned me, I'm pretty sure they thought the same thing. They had me tell my story forward and backward a dozen times."

"You call him Liam?" She looked at me, puzzled.

"Yeah, he said he prefers Liam to Lumberjack."

Mary moved over to the foot of my bed to pet Moo behind the ears. "Then I'm calling him Liam, too. I can't believe he rushed in to save you then actually sat and talked with you."

"What else was he going to do? I was a total mess." I scratched Moo's back as he stretched from one end of the bed to the other.

"I've known him for years, and I don't think he has spoken more than a few sentences."

That was surprising to hear. "Like shy?"

Mary pursed her lips and stared at the ceiling for a few seconds. "No, shy isn't the right word. He's just…" She adjusted her position on the bed, sitting crosswise so she could lean on the side wall. "It's like he was only given a hundred words each day and he wants to use them carefully."

A hard, fast laugh escaped my lips and startled Moo. "That's really poetic, Mary."

She smiled back. "What can I say, I'm a writer." Suddenly her whole face changed. She leapt off the bed and ran from the room, chanting "Oh my gosh" over and over. After a minute she reappeared in the doorway holding a USB stick aloft.

"It's a clue." Then she ran back onto the bed while talking so quickly that I could barely keep up. "For the past few years, instead of going to college, I have been freelance writing for the archery industry so I could stay at home with my mom. I covered tournaments, products, companies, basically anything for the industry. Yesterday, Honey asked if I could do a little bit of editing on her memoir. She gave me this copy. She said there was dirt on everyone, including people here, then she looked around at everyone."

"She said something about that in class, right? I thought she was going to pay someone to write it for her." We shared a quick smile then sobered. "I'm an awful person for saying that." I looked at my lap. Who mocked a dead person?

"Then I'm awful, too. I don't want her dead, but I feel badly that I don't feel worse. You know what I mean? And it is even worse 'cause she was murdered." Moo crawled up into Mary's lap, and she stroked him a few more times then looked at me. "Who did it? Do you think a crazy person could have wandered into the center and killed her?"

"I hope so, but it is a bit of a stretch. Someone would need to either walk from the highway or have the code to the entrance. Then they would need to get a key to the center, and how would they even know Honey would be there? But if it was someone here, then who?"

We sat in silence for a bit, each lost in our own

thoughts. Moo had crawled farther up the bed, and his large block head lay across my lap. I pushed on him but he pushed back. I gave up. "Hey, could you grab that notebook and pen on my desk. We can make a list."

Mary handed them to me and listed off the suspects. "You, me, Tiger, Minx, Owley, Bruce, Liam, and Jess. Is that it?"

I carefully wrote out each name and stared at the list. "Let's add Stranger to the bottom, just in case."

Then I drew a heavy line through my name. Mary leaned over to catch a glance at what I was doing. I angled that list so she could see.

"I crossed myself off the list. I know I didn't do it."

Mary pointed at her name. "Cross me off the list, too."

"Do you have an alibi?" I raised my eyebrows at her.

"No, do you?"

"Okay, okay, I can just rearrange it." I put our names at the bottom and wrote Liam above us. "I don't think Liam did it then stayed in the building. He didn't seem guilty. I can't imagine Jess killing anyone so I'm putting Jess above us. How about putting Tiger at the top? Isn't it usually the lover?"

"He's a good suspect, though I hadn't heard they were dating until Honey said something."

That reminded me of something. "Yesterday when we were partnered up, he said they were a reality couple and put air quotes around reality. I'm going to put Minx under Tiger; she didn't seem to like Honey."

Mary shrugged. "That's just Minx. She gives everyone a hard time. Put Owley below her."

"Why?"

"Honey shot against Owley at the Summer Games during the elimination matches and knocked Owley out of the competition. It was a big upset, because Owley's a much better archer. Maybe Owley is exacting her revenge? Plus, she's just weird."

"Of course, weird." I looked at the new list and compared it to our first one. "Where does Bruce fit? I saw him with Owley, and he snapped at Honey."

Mary's head snapped around to me. "What did they say?"

I shrugged and told her about the interaction I had seen. She leaned forward as I explained, then she blurted out, "You should have told me sooner. Bruce was Honey's coach at the Summer Games, but I heard they weren't working together anymore. I wonder what he told Owley. Maybe he was trying to get her to hire him as a coach."

"Why did Honey stop working with him? Did she fire him?"

"I don't know. Do you think there is something in the memoir about it? I'll be right back."

I looked at the list. I would prefer to think that it was Bruce, Tiger, Owley, or Minx because I knew them the least. Mary was right; the memoir might have a clue as to the motive. I tossed the notebook on my desk and crawled out of bed. Moo stretched out on the now-empty bed and sighed deeply. Neither of us had enough sleep. I felt shaky, and the clothes I had fallen asleep in were sticky and no longer comfortable.

I stepped into the small shared area between our two rooms. It had a TV, a very stiff couch with removable pillows that could double as a bed in a pinch, a chair, and the world's smallest kitchenette. Mary was working on her computer.

"I'm going to hop in the shower real quick. You need to give the memoir to the police."

Mary looked up from her computer. "I'm totally ahead of you on that one. You want me to make you some coffee?"

"You're a saint."

In the shower, I let the hot water run over me until I felt human again. It had been a long time since I had gotten so little sleep; probably not since my ill-fated thirtieth birthday party, when my marriage had officially been destroyed. At least no one had died that night, though I could have killed several someones.

When I emerged from the shower dressed in my most comfortable clothes, Mary was on the phone.

"Oh, she just got out of the shower. We'll be there in a minute."

She handed me a coffee, and I wrapped my hands around the warm cup as she hung up and turned to me.

"Jess wants us to come over as soon as possible. She sounds stressed. Are you ready?"

I slipped on my outside shoes and looked around for the shoes I wore in the center when I realized I had lost them sometime the night before. The oversized boots designed for outdoor work were warm and comfortable but ridiculous for indoor wear. When I had gone to town last week, I had picked them up along with half a dozen pairs of athletic indoor shoes to put on while at work. It was common to take off your shoes at the door and would be required at the center during winter and mud season.

I grabbed a different pair from my room and called Moo to my side.

"I think I'm ready."

Mary grabbed a stack of items off the corner of the counter and opened the door. We stepped out into the chilly morning.

***

As we stepped into the building and slipped into our athletic shoes, we ran into Liam. As he approached, Mary peeled off and headed toward an officer, with the USB containing Honey's memoir in hand. Liam greeted Moo with a head scratch before greeting me.

"How are you feeling today?"

Last night I had been so distracted by Honey being dead that I hadn't fully appreciated Liam's good looks. He was even more handsome in daylight. I suddenly felt shy and took a few seconds to gather my composure by tucking a nonexistent lock of hair behind my ear. "Oh, I think I feel about how you would expect after discovering a murder and getting a few hours of sleep with a beast bedded down on my knees."

Liam chuckled. "I make him sleep on the floor, but once he snuck up on the bed and pushed me off."

We both laughed then stared at Moo. Liam seemed to want to say more, and after a few seconds he hesitantly began. "Be careful. We don't know who killed Honey or why. You and Mary should stay together. I'm taking Moo to my room for breakfast and then grabbing a quick nap, but I'll try to find you later today."

I started to dismiss his concerns, but he interrupted me. His eyes were a little bloodshot, and I couldn't quite tell if they were blue or green. I wanted to lean closer and find out.

"Just be careful. It took us forever to hire a tech person. We can't lose you now."

Mary came back to join us and greeted Liam. "Hey, Liam, I hear that you were a hero last night."

Liam nodded his head back quickly in an acknowledgement at Mary, and just the edges of his mouth moved in the smallest of smiles. Then he gave us a wave and headed out of the center with Moo.

Mary turned to me and smacked my arm. "See? If he strung more than two sentences together when talking to me, I would die of shock. Did he actually talk to you?"

I watched Liam as he walked with Moo bounding along at his side across the parking lot toward the housing units before returning to Mary to reply. "Yeah, he said we should stick together until the police figured out who the killer was. Did you give them the memoir?"

Mary gave me the side eye for a few seconds before answering. "Yep, though they didn't seem convinced that it held any great secrets, plus they quizzed me on where I was last night."

We walked down the hallways toward Jess's office, which was just past Robbie's office. Jess was slumped over her desk, her head hidden beneath a mound of dark curly hair. Her arms were thrown across the desk. A bottle of antacids was knocked over with a few escaped tablets flung over the desk. I tentatively knocked on the door.

"Jess?"

A mumbled wail emerged from under the mountain of hair.

"Mary, can you give Jess and I a few moments to talk privately?"

Mary gave a snort and slid down the wall of the hallway and flipped open her tablet.

I stepped into Jess's office and pulled a chair up to the desk. Reaching over, I patted her hand. "Hey, you okay?"

Jess jerked her head up. I pulled back in shock and let out a small peep of surprise. Her eyes had deep circles under them that were reminiscent of a raccoon—a combination of lack of sleep and smeared mascara. Her hair formed a halo of fuzzy curls all around her head.

Before I could think, I blurted out the first thought in my head. "Good gracious, you're a hot mess."

She glared at me. "Gee, that's helpful, Di. This is the worst day of my life. What am I going to do?" Her breath reeked of berries and coffee. I reeled back, crushing pink-and-purple antacids under my heel.

She belched loudly and finished off the coffee in her mug.

"Hey, hey, it'll be okay." Whether it was true or not, it seemed like the right thing to say, but Jess disagreed.

"How?" she wailed. "I was up late going over the material for today, then suddenly there were cops everywhere. I went outside and they told me there had been a death. The center has only been open for a short time, this was my first big event, then Honey had to get murdered."

"I doubt that was really Honey's fault."

Jess glared at me and continued. "She could have at least had the decency to die later. Who is going to want to come to the murder center now? Everything is ruined. Ruined." Her voice was steadily rising as she spoke. I shushed her as best I could before she got hysterical. She ran her hands through her hair and pulled out an antacid.

I tried to guide the conversation in a more helpful direction. "What are you going to do today?"

"See if New Zealand needs archery coaches? See if I can volunteer for the witness protection program? See if that Mars mission is full already?" She collapsed on her desk again.

"Oh come on, don't you think you are overreacting a bit?"

She looked up at me aghast. "Overreacting? After I called Mary, I had to explain to the owner of Westmound that a Summer Games athlete died at her brand new center. How could this day get any worse?"

I looked at her for a second before quipping back, "At least you aren't Honey."

Jess stared at me then started giggling. The giggling changed to full-blown laughter, and she clutched at her stomach, gasping for air. She wiped her eyes. "Poor

Honey. I'm such an awful person."

I shook my head in sympathy. Honey had made a beautiful corpse. She looked better dead than either Jess or I looked this morning. Her makeup hadn't been smeared, and other than all the blood, her hair was perfect.

She giggled a bit more in a high, hysterical tone. "The rest of the coaches' course is canceled. We already told Minx, Owley, and Tiger. They are being questioned by the police, and apparently they can't leave just yet. The rest of the participants that didn't stay at the center are meeting at a nearby hotel, and I will give them the test on what we covered and reschedule the rest of the course for a later time. If I still have a job at that time. Most of the center is closed. The firearm entrance side, the equipment room all the way to the weight room. Obviously. But this side is open, and I opened both archery ranges, long and short, so Minx, Tiger, and Owley could practice if they want. Plus, the cafeteria is open. I had to fight with the police about that. They don't want us to leave during the investigation, but they wanted to close the cafeteria. We ended up at a compromise; the cooks aren't allowed on site, but we could at least get to the food. Did I hear you say Mary was with you?"

At the sound of her name, Mary popped into the office. "Yep, I'm here."

Jess nodded approvingly. "Good, you two stay together and out of trouble. Go take a nap or something. I swear if anyone else dies, I will kill them."

"Sounds like an effective solution." I gave her cold, clammy hand another pat as I got up to leave.

As Mary and I walked down the hallway toward the cafeteria, I was lost in my thoughts until Mary interrupted me.

"Who do we investigate next?" She was looking down at a notebook with a list of names. It was the list I started earlier in my room.

"What are you talking about? When did you grab that?"

"We have to solve Honey's murder."

I stopped dead, staring at her. After a second, she stopped and stepped back to stand next to me.

She took a deep breath and let it out in a huff before starting. "We are bad people because we're not more upset about Honey's death, right?"

I nodded my agreement. "Yes, we have cold, black hearts."

"But if we solve her murder then we're good people, and it all evens out."

I shook my head. "I don't think that is how it works."

She shook her head at me. "No, no, I gave it a lot of thought while you were in the shower, and this is the only way. You already got Jess's story, so now we just need to go through the rest of the list and read Honey's memoir."

"I thought you gave the USB drive to the police?"

She pulled out the tablet from under the notebook and waggled it at me. "I did but not before I uploaded it. I started it. It's poorly written, but she's right about it having lots of secrets. She threw everyone under the bus, and I've only read a chapter or two. The theme seems to be Honey is awesome and everyone else is a screw-up."

"Why am I not surprised?" I started walking again, and Mary fell in step beside me. "What makes you think we could find the murderer?"

"Simple—we make a great team. You're super smart, and I know everything about archery, plus we have the memoir. And we totally knew who the killer was on the cop show the other night!"

We had bonded our first evening together over a shared love of mystery shows on TV. We unwound after work solving crimes from the small screen, from cop shows to cartoon mysteries. If there was a mystery, we were going to solve it.

I waved a hand at her, dismissing the cop show. "That was just editing and the fact that the most famous guest star is always the killer."

She steamed ahead, unbothered by my assertion. "We'll be like Batman and Robin, solving crimes and stuff."

"Wait, who gets to be Batman?"

"Duh, obviously you are. Batman's way older than Robin."

I stopped dead, mouth agape. "Hey."

At least I was the hero in this scenario.

Mary ignored me and entered the cafeteria. She bee-lined for a table while yelling over her shoulder, "Grab me a bowl of cereal while I plan the investigation. Something sugary, please."

"I don't remember Batman getting the food. Where's Alfred?" Would it be such an awful idea to poke around a bit and find out where everyone was last night?

I carried over two bowls of cereal, with bananas balancing on the crook of each arm. "What does the memoir say?"

"Meh, I'm still in her early years of shooting. She says that when she joined her college team, they were so excited because of her obvious talent and leadership skills that they made her team captain."

My jaw dropped. "Are you serious? I was on that team, and she made the cut because so many seniors had graduated the year before. I don't think anyone thought she was particularly talented. We had never finished lower than third place at any team event, so we weren't relying on a brand-new archer to save us. Jess was the team captain our junior and senior year, not Honey."

Mary swiped on her tablet. "Let me find it. Yes, here it is. 'The team captain was a hysterical junior with awful greasy hair. Everyone thought she was an awful person and an awful archer. They had to make her team captain because otherwise she would cry and cry, but really everyone thought of me as the leader of the team.' Think that is about Jess?"

I sucked air through my teeth. "Holy cow, Honey wasn't looking to make friends, was she? If Jess had read that, she would have killed Honey."

Mary closed the tablet cover. "Do you think Jess did it?"

It was impossible for Jess to have killed someone, but I still gave Mary's question serious thought based on the information we had. "No, and here's why. Honey being killed at the center is going to cause both Jess and Robbie big problems professionally. If Honey was killed somewhere else, then I guess it could be Jess but…" I shrugged my shoulders. "So that isn't really definitive. Huh, what do we do now? I barely slept last night, and I'm about to collapse if we sit much longer."

I gathered up the dishes and took them into the kitchen while Mary yelled after me. "I was going to read Honey's memoir and gather all the clues for us, but I guess we could just wing it. Who do we talk to first, Batman?"

I crossed the room and turned the notebook to read it. "Hmm, Tiger's at the top."

Mary gathered up her stuff and stood up. "No, it couldn't be Tiger. He's too handsome." She let out a sigh and stared off into the distance briefly. "Let's see if someone is at the archery ranges."

I rolled my eyes while grabbing a pen Mary

dropped. "Oh yeah, with investigation skills like that, we'll solve the mystery in no time."

***

We walked past a large bank of windows that looked out over the long archery range. Tiger was set up on a seventy-meter target, which was the standard for outdoor recurve competition. He was alone.

"Seems that fate has decided for us. We can talk to Tiger first. What should we ask?"

Tiger picked up his bow and prepared to shoot another end at the long target. An end in archery is the act of shooting arrows, going to the target to retrieve them, then returning to the shooting line. Tiger had just started a new end.

Mary confidently headed toward the door. "I got this."

By the time we entered, Tiger was at full draw.

Mary burst through the door. "Can we talk to you, Tiger, we're invest—"

I grabbed her arm hard.

Hissing through my teeth, my whisper cut her off. "What are you doing? Did you go to the Mr. Bean School of Investigation? You don't tell him that we are looking for the killer."

Tiger continued to shoot, and Mary's head bobbled between the two of us. "I figured I would just tell him we are looking into the murder and ask where he was."

I rolled my eyes at her. "No, absolutely not. Don't tell anyone what we are doing."

Tiger finished his end of six arrows and put his bow down on the stand. Sauntering over to us, he plopped down on a chair and kicked his legs up on the table.

"Hey ladies, what are you inviting me to?"

In unison, Mary and I said, "What?"

A confused look crossed his face before replying. "You guys came in and said, 'We're inviting' then stopped. Did I not hear you right? I was pretty focused."

I jumped on the opportunity. "Oh, Mary tripped. She's very clumsy."

Mary glared at me.

"We want to invite you to…" To what? Honey just died, we can't have a party. "Invite you to a celebration of Honey's life. Tonight." I smiled broadly at my own brilliance.

"Aww, that's sweet. She was a good kid." Tiger looked down at his hands in his lap and frowned.

I awkwardly patted his shoulder.

"I'm sorry, Tiger, how are you holding up?"

"I feel awful for her. She rubbed a lot of people the wrong way, but she wasn't a bad person, just ambitious." He sighed deeply and covered his face with his hands for a few seconds before dropping them on his lap again. "I want to clear the air about us dating. That wasn't totally true, but she didn't want me to say so. She had some agent tell her that if she wrote a book, they could get her a show, but they needed more than just her. They said she needed an interesting husband or boyfriend and wacky friends, that kinda thing. So she asked me if I could be her boyfriend for the show. I said sure, why not? She was cute enough, and we had a thing once or twice in the past. Plus, I had nothing too serious going on with anyone else. She said it was important that everyone thought we were a real couple, but I told her that you can't cage the Tiger."

He gave us a sad wink, and Mary chuckled softly. His words were flirty, but his tone was sad.

"The agent was probably a scam artist, and Honey was never going to write a book. Who reads books these days? But just in case, I did my best to act like the loyal boyfriend."

I gave a snort. “Loyal boyfriend, eh? Don’t expect to win an Oscar anytime soon.”

“What can I say, my natural charisma is, like, irresistible. Need any help with the thing tonight?”

Mary and I looked at each other and shrugged.

“Have you told everyone? Arranged for liquor so we can toast?” We shook our heads no to Tiger’s questions. “Have you done anything? You two are doing an awful job of planning this.”

“Planning what?” a voice said from behind us. Turning around, I saw Owley entering the range carrying her bow and her quiver hooked over her shoulder.

“Mary and Di are planning a celebration of Honey’s life for tonight, like after dinner?”

“Ya,” I replied, “after dinner is perfect.” I looked at Owley, expecting that she would reply, but she stared at me. I looked at Tiger then Mary then back at Owley. The pressure of the silence weighed heavily on me, and I reached out for any topic.

“I like your shoes,” I blurted. Owley had black athletic shoes on with teal accents. She looked down at the shoes then back at me. Eternity stretched out before she replied.

"Huh?" Her high, thin voice wavered a bit. She shifted her weight between her feet.

"Your shoes are cute. I would totally buy a pair like that." I gave her a big smile, hoping that the compliment would prompt a response.

"Um, Di, I think you bought the same pair last week." Mary had gone shopping with me and would know.

I laughed, loud and awkward, in the large empty room (and feeling like a total idiot). "No wonder I like them. We could be shoe twins."

Tiger and Mary gave a tiny laugh, but Owley continued to stare. Finally she replied, "I need to practice." She walked over to the shooting line, put her bow down next to Tiger's, and started getting her equipment on.

"Hey, great, good luck. Mary and I have things to do." I gave Tiger a quick wave and dragged Mary from the range.

***

Once in the hallway, I reared around to face Mary. I kept my voice down. "We need to figure out a better way to talk to people. I don't want anyone knowing that we are investigating."

“Batman does, you know, in the movie.” Mary lowered her voice and said, “I am Batman.”

I chuckled but blew out an exasperated sigh while rubbing my forehead. “We’re not Batman and Robin. At best, we’re Laurel and Hardy.”

“Oh, sorry I couldn’t match the brilliance of your investigation, Miss-I-Like-Your-Shoes.”

At the far end of the hallway, a police officer was watching us. I gave him a big smile and waved then started walking toward the entrance. “Fair enough, neither of us is good at winging it. As much as it pains me, I think you’re right. Let’s go back to the room. You can read the memoir, and I can take a short nap before my head explodes.”

***

A dancy little electronic tune woke me up. I grabbed my phone and cleared my throat. “Hello,” I croaked.

“It’s me. Jess. Are you in your room? I need to introduce you to someone. Don’t move.” It all came out in a tumble of words.

“Sure, come on over.” I looked at the phone, but Jess had already ended the call. I rubbed my eyes and took in the surroundings. I was lying on the couch in the middle room of our unit. Mary was on the floor, working at the coffee table with her computer, tablet, notebook and a variety of pens spread out in front of her. I had closed my eyes for just a second when a knock on the door broke the silence again.

"Come in," I called out as I swung my feet onto the floor. Jess entered, buzzing with excitement. Following behind her was a beautiful, tall lady dressed in an impeccable outfit. Her stance reminded me of many a CEO I had met in California, confident and observant. Her eyes landed on Mary, and she greeted her. "Hello, Mary, how is your mother?"

"Very good, thank you for asking."

Jess gestured at me. "This is Di. Di, this is the owner of Westmound Industries, Mrs.—"

But the lady stepped around her and extended her hand while saying, "Call me Elizabeth, please. We are all part of the Westmound family."

I stood up, wishing I had bothered to look in the mirror before they arrived, and shook Elizabeth's hand. She had a strong grip.

"I wish I could have met you under better circumstances. I came over as soon as I was notified. Liam says that you found Honey. How are you doing?"

I had heard that Westmound headquarters was in Utah; she must have driven over first thing this morning.

"I was pretty upset, but Liam was very kind."

"I'll be making arrangements for a grief counselor to come to the center and talk to everyone as soon as possible."

I waved a hand in the air. "Oh no, I'm fine." I smiled brightly while Elizabeth studied my face.

"Do you mind if I sit for a second?" As I nodded, she sat in a chair and gestured to the couch for me to sit before continuing. "Do you know that I personally made the final decision on every person hired for the center? This center is really my pride and joy. I love the entire outdoor industry, but I have a special place in my heart for archery. You were the final hire we made, and I did some internet research on you. We're very lucky to have you here."

I fidgeted in my seat. I knew there was quite a bit about me available online, from articles about high-dollar contracts our company earned to a few about women in technology and at least one article about me leaving the company when divorce proceedings started. I silently begged that she not ask about the divorce.

"Thank you, I'm happy to be here."

"About ten years ago, my husband and father passed away in the same year. I was left to run both growing companies. I insisted that I was fine and had everything under control. Eventually my son quit college to come home and help me. He made me go and talk to someone, and I think that was the only thing that saved me. There is no shame in letting someone in." She smiled at me with genuine warmth.

I smiled back. "Thank you."

"If you ever need anything, please don't hesitate to tell Jess or Liam. Or you can call me directly."

As she headed to the door she asked Jess to show her where Liam's room was. They said goodbye to us and left.

Mary gushed from her spot on the floor.

"She's so awesome. I did a couple articles on her and Westmound companies in general last year. She's one of the few female owners in the industry. She knows everyone by first name, even if you met her once five years ago, and she pays attention to every company she owns and employee she has. She must not sleep. Plus, she has been so kind to me. That's part of the reason I applied to work here. I want to be her when I grow up," Mary said in an awestruck tone.

"I think I do, too. I can't believe she took the time to come by the room. She probably has a lot of other stuff on her mind right now." I gazed at the door. "How long was I asleep?" I was still exhausted, but I no longer felt like death warmed over.

"A couple of hours, but I have good news. I finished reading the memoir. Even being super careful to read every word, it was still really short. I highlighted some stuff to read to you. Honey didn't exactly tell the truth in a lot of the stories."

"Like what?" I dragged the notebook over the table and starting looking at her notes.

"It's hard to explain. She didn't flat-out lie about any facts, like winning a medal she didn't or making a team she didn't, but every story is just a bit off. Let me back up. You didn't know much about Honey, right? Can I tell you from the beginning?"

I smiled and grabbed a pen to doodle with while Mary talked. Mary loved to tell a story. I had avoided personal stories from either of us, and she respected that, but she gave me long-winded explanations about every show we watched.

"Honey was spoiled. I don't know how rich her

parents were, but they had some connections and enough money that she could devote herself to full-time training. In her book, she talks about being a triumphant winner and a gracious loser, but that wasn't the case. She had a reputation for being a poor sport: not shaking hands after a match, being rude if she lost, just unpleasant, but nothing really against the rules."

Mary got up off the floor and sat in a chair to continue.

"Nationwide, we only have about a hundred women that are seriously training in competitive recurve archery. The talent pool is good but not very deep. Honey had been sitting in about eighth position of the national rankings for years: very consistent but not good enough."

I was boggled by her exact statement. "How do you know that?"

"Because of the articles I wrote. Normally I'm a freelancer, but this last summer I worked part time with NOUSAA, the National Organization of USA Archery, writing little articles about the teams for the Summer Games. Everyone else on the team was easy. Owley lives and dies archery. I don't think I have even heard of her dating until today, but I will get to that later."

I drew a heart next to Owley's name in the notebook.

"Owley trains nonstop, and this was already her second Summer Games. She's our top-ranked female and places well internationally, though she tends to be a bit unpredictable. One world event she will medal, then the next she won't even make top thirty. She may be pretty weird in person, but she sounds great on paper."

"What about Minx?" I had taken an instant dislike to her abrasive personality.

"Minx is awesome, a real great story. She comes from this huge family, has like a million sisters. They don't have a lot of money. She lives at home and helps with the family business during the day then trains in the evening. They have bake sales on the weekend to raise enough money to send her to tournaments. She's a rising star in the organization. She has been on a steady climb for the past few years, and she will probably eventually be better than Owley. She's tough and a hard worker. If she gets into the OSA program here to train full time, she might be unstoppable. If I had been in charge of publicity, I would have had Minx everywhere, but I found something that explained why she wasn't. I'll pull it up for you."

"Argh, she gets under my skin. And Honey?" I attempted to draw a skull and crossbones next to Minx's name.

"Honey's story was really hard to write. She only barely made the team at all. The team was picked over three events, and her ranking coming in was sixth. There were only three spots on the team, but it wasn't the best year for our athletes. There isn't much money in recurve archery, especially for females, so a couple of long-time athletes retired when they got great job offers or got married. Two others got pregnant, and another had to leave the first event when her mom was rushed to the hospital."

"How sad. Did her mom die?"

"No, she lived, but if you miss one event you can't advance." She thumbed through the tablet.

"That sucks, but at least she didn't lose her mom as well." It would be too awful.

"I totally agree; there'll be other Summer Games. I got hired right before the final trial so I went to watch. Minx and Owley had the top two places pretty well locked up, but Honey barely snuck in third by a fraction of a point. She hasn't won a single national medal in her ten years of shooting, never competed internationally or anything. No hobbies. Nothing. It was a super boring article. That's why I did so much research on her; I was hoping that something would come up."

"You make it sound like she didn't deserve to make the team. Do you think she cheated or something?"

I felt as though I was missing something to the story.

"No, she didn't cheat, at least as far as I know. She just made it sound like she earned all these things when really it was more about other people's misfortunes or her using money or influence to pull strings."

"Didn't she place the highest at the Summer Games?"

"That was super surprising. I read something in her memoir that was weird about that—" Mary was cut off abruptly by a knock at the door.

CHAPTER FIVE

Mary got up to answer the door. As she opened it, a black nose pushed inside, and Moo ran into the room. He hopped up on the couch next to me as Minx entered the room, holding two arrows and a baggie.

"Liam has a meeting at the center and asked if I could drop the dog off here. I need to fletch two arrows, and the equipment room at the center is still off limits. Do y'all have some acetone and alcohol?"

Mary came back and swiped across her tablet while answering Minx, "Sure, give me just a second and I can grab it for you. Here, Di, this is that article I was telling you about." She handed me the tablet before she left the room.

She had pulled up a section from Honey's memoir. I scanned the page, focusing on a few highlighted sentences. The page started with her returning home after the trials. She mentioned getting headshots, hiring a publicist, getting her hair cut, speaking to sponsors about renegotiating her contracts, and talking to new sponsors but very little about practicing. Mary had highlighted a line. "I wanted to make the most of my one opportunity."

Minx and Mary returned to the room, and I shut the tablet cover and notebook. Minx settled on the floor with a small trash can next to her.

"Hey, Princess, what article you reading?" Minx leaned back on her hands and smirked at me. She had emphasized the word princess and appeared to be waiting for my reply.

"Princess?" My suspicions were increased when her smirk burst into a full-blown smile. I had taken the bait.

"Yeah, Princess Di. I figured that you needed a pro name, and I'm pretty good at them, right Mary?" She nodded her head in Mary's direction but watched me for my reaction.

Mary squealed with glee and clapped her hands once. "Princess Di. It's perfect."

I didn't like being called Princess. It might be okay

for a father to call his daughter that, but in an adult it carried the implications of spoiled and high maintenance. "Why in the world would I need a pro name? I'm not a professional archer."

My tone held a bit more force and snip than I intended, which made Minx smile wider.

"I saw you shooting yesterday. Honey said that you used to compete in college and then you took a job here. It's only a matter of time. I've an eye for these things." Minx sat forward and wiped her hands on her pants then started cleaning her arrows. She peeled the tiny plastic veins off along with the black tape that held them on.

"Did you see that in Honey?" I needed to take control of this conversation.

"Geez, Honey." She stopped to look at me. "I heard you guys are throwing a celebration of life or something for her. How did you get sucked into that?"

I shrugged noncommittally, hoping that she wouldn't ask for more details, then countered, "Not a fan?"

"Were you?" Minx didn't even look up, but I could see a half smile on her face. Was it possible that she was being difficult on purpose? I looked at Mary then tipped my head in Minx's direction.

As Mary and I silently communicated, Minx used a combination of acetone on a cotton ball and her thumbnail to work that double-sided tape off of the arrow shaft.

"Minx, I was just telling Di about the Summer Games and writing those articles about you guys. Yours was the most fun."

Mary smiled at Minx with genuine warmth, and Minx returned it.

"Thanks, you did a great job on it. Though really it wasn't much competition, was it? Honey had that whole team of people helping her, but even they couldn't make her likable. Owley has no personality. That's part of the reason I'm here. She has been in the range, watching videos of her competing against Honey in the Summer Games Elimination match for the past hour or two. Owley sitting there with those big, empty eyes watching, watching, watching. I was about to go mad."

"I heard Honey had a lot of people supporting her." I put finger quotes around supporting.

Minx snorted with a flash of amusement in her eyes.

"Right, supporting her." She echoed my finger

quotes. "People have gone into space with a smaller support crew. After the Summer Games team was selected in the fall we had a lot of team events to meet the coaches, familiarize ourselves with shooting together for the team event, publicity, etc. NOUSAA kept pushing team America, but Honey was all about Honey. She wanted to have her own personal photographer for every photo op, and we were always standing around waiting on someone." Minx was focused on scrubbing the arrow.

I gave Mary a nod to encourage her. Minx was responding better to Mary than me. "I always wondered why she got so many stories done on her when you and Owley were better archers."

"Simple—money. Mary, you and NOUSAA did a great job trying to support us, but you had six athletes, including the men. Honey just had more resources. Her publicist could get out more specialized information faster, and they had connections. And she didn't believe in sharing the spotlight at all. She didn't even pretend."

"That sounds frustrating," I said.

"Frustrating? It was infuriating." Minx put down her arrows to look at me fully. "I had spent years shooting and training for this opportunity, and Honey turned it into a living nightmare. I was a background player in her play. Do you know that she brought an analyst in to assess her competition, including us? Originally, she told all of us that the analyst was looking at other countries. But we're archers, not basketball or football players. Everyone has the same game plan: aim at the middle, and try to hit the middle. Sure, some people are weaker in the rain or wind, but unless we invented weather control, what good would it do to know that? Then it came out that the analyst was also looking at Owley and me. Looking for weaknesses. The team manager about flipped out. They kicked everyone out of the camp and all future training camps except the athletes and one personal coach each. It was glorious."

Mary leaned forward. "How did I not know this?"

Minx grabbed the alcohol to swab down the now-clean arrows and prep them for new vanes. "They kept it pretty quiet and asked us as a favor not to say anything. I plan to be around for a long time and could use some favors in my pocket. That was the root of Honey's problem; she never thought long term."

That reminded me of the phrase that Mary had highlighted in the memoir. I tried to catch Mary's eyes, but she was ahead of me. "I heard somewhere that

Honey thought this was her only shot at making a Summer Games team. Like she had to make the most of it."

"Yes, exactly. The Summer Games only come around once every four years, and she only made the team this year because better archers couldn't." She gave Mary a tight, thin smile. "She never loved archery like most archers do. I love competing, practicing, hanging with other archers, talking about equipment, competition, or archers, and just being at the range. It's like a second home to me. But Honey wasn't interested in any of that. She saw archery as a stepping stone to something bigger or better."

For once I had something I could add to the conversation. "You know I went to college with her? When she joined the archery team, she said she chose archery because it was the easiest sport to pick up and be world class at. That really rubbed people wrong. We loved archery and obsessed about it every second, but she acted like it was so easy that even an idiot could do it."

Minx gave me a smile, and for a moment I thought we shared an understanding. Then she opened her mouth. "If you loved archery so much in college, why did you leave?"

An uncomfortable, at least for me, silence descended on the room. I tried to stutter out my go-to response. "Oh, you know how life gets in the way and stuff." I avoided her eyes.

Minx squinted at me and started to reply. "Oh come on, what does that even—"

Mary cut her off. "What did Honey think the Summer Games was a stepping stone to?"

Minx looked at me then Mary then back to me. She rolled her eyes then finally turned back to Mary. "Fame? Fortune? A rich husband? She was sure that she would become famous, like that reality show she mentioned yesterday. She figured that she was like those ice skaters, snowboarders, or even the speed skater that hosts a game show. She would dance with the stars or be on a variety of celebrity shows. She was a total nut job if she thought archery was going to make her famous. Archery is awesome, but we are a long way from being considered celebrities."

Mary tilted her head to the side. "So she wanted to have a reality show about her shooting archery?"

"No, she wanted a reality show *instead* of shooting archery." Minx was fletching her arrows by carefully placing double-sided tape on pencil lines she had drawn on the arrows then attaching thin plastic vanes to the tape and pressing down firmly. "She was always talking about her future plans. Television, inspirational speaking, maybe a few coaching seminars. None of us really cared; we were focused on the Summer Games and competition. She was always blah blah blah, but I got pretty good at tuning her out."

"Did she bug Owley, too?" Mary got up to grab a small bottle of glue to hand to Minx, who put a drop on the leading edge of each fletching.

"Yes, but kind of opposite of me. If Honey got on my nerves about stuff, I would just tell her to shut up, then I would just move on. Owley never said anything to Honey, and things would fester. I never noticed Honey when I was shooting; I was in my own little world. Owley, on the other hand, would complain to me if Honey stood too close to her on the line or mumbled under her breath. I told her to say something to Honey, but she wouldn't. Sometimes I would tell Honey to back off for her, but I'm not the archery police."

"What was Bruce like? I didn't realize that he used to be Honey's coach until Mary told me this morning. I only know him as a coworker." I ventured back into the conversation on what I hoped was a safe topic.

"What do you think of him?" She threw back the question at me and cocked an eyebrow. She kept making these digs at me, but this time I could answer in fullness.

"He seems nice enough. Other than saying hi in the hallways or nodding at meals, I have only really encountered him twice. The first was a meeting where he explained his responsibilities at the center and what he needed from me. He was distracted and snapped a few times. The other time was yesterday at the coaches' training. I didn't talk to him."

I thought about what I had seen while waiting to pick out a bow. "Are he and Owley close? Did he have a falling out with Honey? I saw him talking to Owley privately and snapping at Honey."

Minx gave her arrows one last spin then set them on the coffee table.

"Finally, you are adding something to this conversation, Princess. I don't know what was going on with Honey and Bruce. Bruce is a cool guy, always polite to me even though we never worked together. He seemed to do his best for Honey while not stepping on anyone's toes, unlike a lot of coaches. But at the

Summer Games, he and Honey must have had a falling out. Right after Honey and Owley's match, he disappeared and I didn't see him again. Honey didn't seem to care. We asked where he went, and she said he was a stick in the mud and left."

I chewed on that thought. What could have happened during the match to cause such a rift between the two?

"My arrows are all done. Have you guys eaten? Let's go grab some food." Minx stood up. It sounded deceptively like a question but with the forcefulness of a command.

We hadn't eaten since breakfast. "Sure, but let me change. I fell asleep in my clothing, again, and I feel gross."

***

I grabbed some stuff and went into the bathroom to run a washcloth over my face and skin. The whole process helped me to feel fully awake and ready. Moo followed me in the bathroom and wedged his face into the sink to drink from the faucet. When he was sated, he stepped back and swiped his mouth across my pants, leaving an immense wet spot. "Oh, Moo."

I shooed him out of the bathroom and went to

change into drop pants. I took a few seconds to drop my parents a message on the computer, with only the vaguest of details. I would have to call them soon to tell them the whole story once I knew the whole story.

I stepped into the middle room to tell Mary and Minx I was ready but was startled to see Moo standing in the middle of the room with a black T-shirt on. Emblazoned across his back was the iconic Batman logo.

Mary was standing proudly behind him. "It's Batdog."

Minx snorted from the couch.

I looked at them then back at Moo. "Where did you get that?"

"It's mine."

I rolled my eyes. "Take it off him, and let's get going."

Mary rushed over and ran her hands over the shirt. "No, it stays. He likes it."

"I'm not sure I'm ready to be the type of lady who dresses her dog." I stared at Moo dubiously, but he pranced around the room. Suddenly, he lifted to nose to the sky and let out an extended "woo" while dancing. He pounced onto the floor, his paws straight out and wide, his chest brushing the floor while his rump waggled back and forth high in the air.

Minx got up and opened the door, and Moo hopped up to rush out. "Batdog has made his decision. Y'all coming or not?"

With a shrug, I followed them out. Mary grabbed her notebook and tablet, then we headed to the center across the parking lot.

***

The cafeteria was off limits to Moo, but just next to it was a more casual seating area separated by a half wall with tables and booths for eating or hanging out. This area was open all day, even when the cafeteria was closed. Of course, right now, the cafeteria was unlocked while the staff was gone. Someone had hung up a sign saying "Celebration of Honey's life and career 6:00 p.m. Liquor provided." I went to grab a sandwich then joined Mary and Minx. They had spread out in a booth, legs crossed on the long seats. I sat at a nearby table after grabbing the tablet and notebook from next to Mary.

I bit into my sandwich and turned open the page, angling myself so Minx couldn't see the page. Minx and Mary were discussing next year's archery season and which events were required for National Rankings and debating the value of the Field and Indoor national tournaments.

Mary took a bite of her sandwich and started talking around it. "How can you not love Indoor Nationals? It's just you and your bow. No wind, no weather, no excuses. It really is pure archery."

"Ew, gross, how about not talking with your mouth open, you pig." Minx laughed and threw a wadded-up napkin at Mary. "Indoor archery is cool, but even one bad arrow throws you out of the race. Plus, there is no challenge. Field archery, on the other hand has everything: hills, estimating distances, rocks that destroy arrows if you miss, trees partially obscuring your view, uneven footing, and it always rains. Plus, you are out in nature—what can beat that?"

"What am I? A bear? What do I care about being out in nature?"

They were happily wrapped in their own discussion. I shifted my attention to the notebook and tablet. We had accomplished nothing so far except to confirm that Tiger was a flirt, Minx was not my fan, Owley had nice shoes, and Moo was on a slippery slope of cosplay. I looked over the list and ran through the conversations we had already had, trying to piece out everything that was said and if any of it was more important than we had first thought.

"So, what's next?" I looked up at Mary. Minx must have already left, as we were alone.

"I don't know. This is nothing like the TV shows." I flopped my head down on the table.

"Di?" Mary's hand gently patted my shoulder. "Are you feeling a bit tired?"

I closed my eyes against the cool tabletop, and the couple of hours from last night and the couple-hour nap late this morning added up to a couple of couples, definitely not a full night's sleep. I sat up and scrubbed my face.

"Yeah, and my brain is kinda mushy. I know we need to talk to Bruce about whatever happened with Honey at the Summer Games and whatever happened here when he took Owley into the hallway after snapping at Honey. Plus whatever you found in the memoir. And… whatever." I was babbling. I got up and did some stretches, hoping the movement would wake up my sluggish mind.

Mary pulled out a chair and started looking through her notes.

"I wanted to tell you earlier about a section I read

in the memoir. Most of her notes about the Summer Games were who she met that was famous, interviews and photo ops she had or compliments she got. In fact, the qualifying round had very little details until the last arrow. Here is what it said: 'I knew that if I got a seven or worse on this final arrow that I would have to shoot against Owley. I could feel the wind on my skin and the sun on my face. I raised the bow, and right as I shot, a gust of wind lifted the arrow and it hit a six. I tried to stay happy, but I am just devastated.' See?"

I did a couple of jumping jacks, thinking about what she shared. "I don't see much other than the fact that she needed an amazing editor. 'I am just devastated'? Way to hop around tenses."

"That's part of the problem. She wasn't devastated, then or now. We did an interview afterwards, and she was so happy. I don't think she was that great of an actor. In that interview she said she must have bumped the sight, nothing about the wind. Plus, have you heard anything about her that makes you think she really cared about her teammates?"

I stopped mid-jumping jack to think through everything I knew about Honey. "You're right. So I guess she was lying to sound more sympathetic? She didn't seem to have that much self-awareness." I bent over to touch my toes and let the blood flow to my brain.

"It's possible, but you missed the other part that's important. 'I knew that if I got a seven or worse on this final arrow that I would have to shoot against Owley.' How did she know that a seven or worse was what she needed?" Mary carefully wrote out two questions in her notebook. "Was Honey devastated?" and "Did she know she needed a 7 or worse?"

"Could she have added that later to be dramatic? You said she embellished all the stories." Moo started pawing at my dangling arms, so I sat down to scratch his ears.

"I looked back through the article I wrote for the Summer Games, and there was a quote from her saying that her first words to Bruce when stepping off the line was something like 'I'm shooting against Owley tomorrow.'"

I shrugged my shoulders. "So she knew right then. I don't get what the big deal is. She would just have to… wait, how would she know?"

"Thank you, you finally caught up. I have no idea how she knew all that. They have live score updates but only after each end of six arrows. But she would need to be making a bracket while watching her standings and Owley's standings. Someone would need to watch all the arrows that final end, keep track of the score. There is just no way that I can think of that she could do all of that alone."

"And why?" Moo rolled on his back, and I gave his gigantic belly a rub. "Why all that work just to go against Owley?"

"She got national coverage. They could only really cover one match live, and since there were two US competitors in the same match it was a guarantee that she would be on TV."

"Plus, she won," I added.

"She did, and that was a huge upset. Honey shot her average despite a cold, but Owley was a mess. She was all over the target, she was letting down all the time, which isn't typical for her, and she was in tears by the end. It wasn't Owley's best performance."

"Could Honey have caused that? Paid off Owley? Put something in her water? Something? It would all fit perfectly."

Mary perked up. "It would. Owley could totally have killed Honey if that was true. Who could blame her?"

I wiped my hands on my pants, knocking off the black-and-white dog's hair on my dark jeans, and stood up. "How do we prove it?"

Mary pointed out the two questions she had written in her notebook. "Let's start by proving that she purposefully sandbagged in the qualifications to go against Owley. Bruce was the only other person there."

Moo hopped up and started dancing around.

"Hey, Batdog, you wanna go interrogate a potential villain?" He was always up for an adventure. "If I'm Batman, you're Robin, and Moo's Batdog, then Bruce is who?" I thought of his shorter height and overall body shape. Mary and I answered in unison. "The Penguin!"

***

We walked down the hallway and peeked in Bruce's office. He was sitting in his office, whistling and looking happier than I had seen him since I had worked there. Mary passed me the notebook, and I looked at the two questions she had written.

"Hey Bruce, I wanted to ask you if it is true that after Honey finished qualifications she said she was going to shoot against Owley."

His whistling stopped and eyes narrowed. "Yes."

Looking at the next question I asked, "How did she know that she needed a seven or less in order to shoot against Owley?" I didn't look up for a second, but then his heavy breathing filled the silence.

His face was red, his eyes flashed with anger, and his mouth was pursed. His nostrils flared as he huffed through his nose. For a second, I thought he was going to charge me like a bull. Instead, he started bellowing. "I don't know what kind of accusation you're trying to make, but get out of my office."

His voice rose, and little flecks of spit flew from his mouth. I held up my hands to defend myself against his verbal attack. I coughed as the smell of garlic overwhelmed me. He must have eaten the center's entire stock of garlic sausage for lunch.

"Bruce, you can't talk to us like that. We work together; we're going to see each other every day." I was both concerned and confused.

"Not for long. I will not… work anywhere… where…" He was gasping for air while he yelled. A grimace took over his face. His hand fisted into his chest, and he doubled over.

"Are you having a heart attack? Sit down." I raced over to help him into the chair.

He collapsed into the seat and covered his face with his hands.

His shoulders heaved, but his breathing slowed down. "I can't. I just can't anymore. I thought with Honey gone that no one would ever find out, but the guilt is killing me. "

Mary walked over and patted his shoulder. "It's okay, Bruce." Her voice was gentle, slow, and quiet. "Did you kill Honey?"

He shook her hand off his shoulder. Pulling a stained handkerchief out of his pocket, he ran it over his face and blew his nose. "No, I didn't, but she deserved it. It couldn't have happened to a more deserving person. She's evil. She did whatever she wanted and didn't care who it hurt. She threatened to destroy my career, my life's work, if I didn't shut up. There was nothing I could do to stop her anyway. I tried to stay quiet, but it wasn't right."

He sat there, staring straight ahead, muttering, "Not right," under his breath.

I caught Mary's eye. "I think we broke the Penguin."

Mary looked at me, her mouth forming a perfect half circle frown, and nodded. I gestured to the chairs, and we sat down. I opened my mouth a few times, debating how to start.

"Bruce?" I waited for him to look at me before continuing. "I think everyone knew that Honey was only out for herself. It seems to be pretty common knowledge. Maybe the situation isn't as bad as you think."

He blew out a long breath and looked down at his hands. Looking up suddenly, he snapped his shoulders back.

"Right, I'm done. First, you need to know that Honey and I never clicked. I did my best to be a good coach for her and support her, but she often pushed back against my advice. Especially anything that involved hard work. She was always looking for a shortcut. As the Summer Games got closer, she seemed even less into training, but I couldn't make her take advantage of the great opportunity. I had already applied for the job here."

The color in Bruce's face was starting to look healthy, and he sat taller.

"The first thirty-six arrows of qualifying were pretty standard. Her score was right where she had been, and everything was normal. There was a short break, and then we started the next scoring round, and everything changed. Her scores started slipping, but when I tried to talk to her, she would wave me off. She didn't seem upset by her scores dropping, but she was checking this phone she got for international travel and was very focused on that. She started hiding it in her quiver pouch and would put her finger tab in there, check the phone, then pull the tab back out. I told her to get her head in the game, but she told me that she had it under control. That last end, when she shot the six, she stepped off the line and threw her arms around me and squealed like she had won a gold medal. That is when she said that she was shooting against Owley the next day."

Mary was leaning forward, following his every word. Her brows were knit together tight.

"Someone was telling her the rankings and scores. Who?"

"No idea. Her family, one of the people she hired, basically anyone present could have done it. I didn't even realize that she set it up on purpose until the next day."

"What happened?" I leaned forward in my seat.

"Honey makes this big show about having a cold."

Mary startled in her seat. "Yes, I remember that. I just mentioned it to Di this afternoon."

"She made sure everyone knew about this cold on the day of the elimination matches. Her first match is Owley, just like she had said the day before. The first end for score, Owley raises her bow, hits her anchor, and Honey makes a soft *cough cough* noise. Owley let down, then Honey shot. Owley shot and hit a seven, which was unusual. Then the last arrow of the end was the same. Owley gets to full draw, *cough cough*, Owley lets down then shoots badly. I was shocked. The first time she did it, I thought it could possibly be deliberate, but after the second time I *knew* she was messing with Owley on purpose. Honey won that end and got two points."

"Two points? Do I not know how elimination matches are done?" I looked between Mary and Bruce.

Mary waved a hand at me. "They changed them a few years ago to sexy them up. Each end you shoot three arrows. Whoever wins that end gets two points. If you lose, you get zero, and if you tie, then you each get one point. You keep going until someone gets six points. If you both tie at six points, then it is a single-arrow shoot off. Got it?"

"Yeah, yeah. So Honey was cheating?"

Mary responded before Bruce could. "No, there is nothing in the rules about that kinda stuff."

Bruce blustered. "But it is bad sportsmanship. True athletes win through superior effort, not mind games."

"And you could say that Owley wasn't the superior athlete if a little coughing distracted her." Mary sat back, having made her point.

"It didn't seem to be just the coughing so much as letting down. If she let down, then her next shot would be poor. Otherwise, she was nailing the gold. I have no idea how Honey knew, but she used it to her advantage. I begged her to just focus on her own game, but she said if I didn't leave her alone to win she would tell everyone that I told her to do it."

"*Ohhh.*" Mary dragged out the word in realization.

I looked between Mary and Bruce, waiting for an explanation of why it would be different. Bruce finally spoke up.

"First off, I'm not the kind of coach that would encourage head games ever. As a coach, it would be an even bigger deal to be accused of being behind it, because it would make other archers nervous around me. Who would want to ever attend a camp or training session with me in the future if they thought I would use their weaknesses against them in a future match? Even the archers who play mind games don't brag about it."

He ran a hand through his hair, causing tufts to stick up in every direction.

"NOUSAA would not be happy either. Funding and sponsorships were based on our performance at the Summer Games. If Owley had won, she very likely could have gone several more matches, but instead Honey was crushed the next match. Poor Owley, I felt so awful for her. I pulled her aside yesterday to tell her that I noticed that she didn't recover very well after she let down. She said she already knew."

"I think I saw you talking to her. At the range? In the afternoon?"

Bruce nodded.

"I saw you snap at Honey. What did you say?"

Bruce chuckled. "I told her, 'Get out of my way, Spawn of Satan.'"

I snickered at the image of him saying that. Bruce was so straightlaced. The meeting I had with him last week to discuss his department's needs had made this quality evident. He had been very exact about rules, procedure, and liabilities. "How in the world did you and Honey end up working together?"

Again, Bruce looked uncomfortable. He avoided my eyes and refocused on his hands.

"Oh for goodness' sake, how many secrets do you have?" I blurted out.

"It's no secret, at least not his part of the story," Mary corrected. "Bruce was a college archery coach, and three members of the team were caught cheating in a class. Bruce had nothing to do with it. Why are you sensitive about that? He left, and that is when he started coaching Honey. She had blown through a half dozen coaches since I had known her. Would you be shocked to hear that she was high maintenance?"

I snorted in reply. "I'd be shocked if she wasn't."

"Honey wanted her coach to be with her every second and only pay attention to her. That made it impossible for them to work with other students, and eventually they would part ways. She had been on the lookout for a new coach for a while. So how did she convince you to take her on?"

Bruce blew out a deep breath before starting in. "I was only vaguely familiar with her. The collegiate circuit has their own set of tournaments mostly. I left the university job and was looking for another job. I knew they were building this center but it would be a year until it was ready. Honey came to me practically crying that no one would help her and that she only needed me through the Summer Games. It started out okay but it only got worse. I wanted to back out, but I felt guilty about leaving her hanging before such an important event."

"That sure bit you in the butt." I shook my head, feeling sorry for the guy.

"Puh-lease." Mary drew out the single syllable into two long ones. "You're blowing this way out of proportion. Everyone knew Honey and wouldn't doubt for a minute that it was all her idea. You are worrying about nothing. Go talk to Jess. I'm sure she'll agree."

For the first time since we had started talking, Bruce looked genuinely happy. A broad smile broke across his face, revealing a speck of pepper lodged between two teeth. "You really think so?"

"Totally. I mean, a few people might doubt you, you know that already, but anyone who matters won't care. You're just being too sensitive."

Bruce picked up the phone and started dialing. "Excuse me, ladies."

Mary and I got up to leave just as Bruce started speaking into the phone. "Jess, this is important. Can we meet in your office and talk?"

CHAPTER SIX

Moo led the way down the hallways from Bruce's office to mine. He waited patiently for me to unlock the door then entered and curled up on his bed. Mary and I plopped down into chairs. Finally, we had some solid evidence.

"Clearly we can move Bruce to the top of the list." I grabbed the notebook.

"Why? I'm telling you, no one is really going to believe that he forced Honey to play head games. That was such a Honey thing to do." Mary rolled her eyes at me.

"You're right, but that doesn't matter. Bruce thought it would ruin his career, and that's motive for murder. He was ready to throw himself off a bridge when we even asked about Honey purposely sandbagging during qualification. Or throw us off a bridge. We forgot to ask where he was during the murder."

"Oh, good point. I told you we could do this." She reached over and started flipping through the tablet again.

I drew a big arrow next to Bruce's name to the top of the list. I still felt badly for him. He had a very strong stance on playing head games, and it must have been awful to be caught in the middle of them. "Would you really play head games with someone to win a match?"

Mary looked up at me. "Me? No. But I know people who have done it. I don't. I have a strict rule my mom taught me. Eyes on your own paper, like in school, ya know? I focus on my shooting and my game. I think in the long run you have to do that to be successful."

Mary had these moments of pure brilliance that blew me away, especially for her age. She had to be about ten years younger, but sometimes she seemed so much more mature.

"I assume we will want to talk to Owley next. We need to see what she knows about this. Did she know that Honey messed with her head? How mad was she about getting knocked out? Minx said that Honey gave Owley a hard time; maybe Owley snapped and killed her."

"Could be; she has those freaky eyes." We looked at each other and made our eyes as big as possible then giggled as we collected our stuff again to go find Owley, which turned out to be a short search, as Minx, Owley and Tiger were in the long range across the hall.

Minx and Tiger were shooting at seventy meters, their arrows arcing through the air, and the twin thumps of the arrows impacting the target mats carried through the air of the quiet range. We gave them a head nod of acknowledgement and passed them to go to the far wall, which Owley was sitting against. A computer was in her lap, and she was hugging a wall outlet at least twenty yards from where Tiger and Minx were shooting. I kept Moo close to me since he wasn't technically allowed on any of the ranges.

Mary slid down the wall next to Owley and asked, "Whatcha watching?"

I sat opposite them and crossed my legs, fidgeting on the hard floor.

Owley stared at the screen, never making eye contact with either of us. "The match between Honey and me at the Summer Games."

Mary and I exchanged a quick glance. That is what Minx said Owley was doing hours earlier. "Again?"

Owley barely nodded her head. "The video is almost an hour. I had to watch it to be sure."

Mary gently put her hand on Owley's left hand. "Are you okay? To be sure of what?"

Owley pulled her eyes off the screen and looked at Mary. "She did it on purpose. She was coughing on purpose when I was at full draw. Look."

I scooted up to Owley's other side and looked at the screen. She had a tiny Post-it with time stamps written on it. She scrolled to one of them and pressed Play.

The footage showed Owley, and behind her, Honey. Right as Owley drew up and hit her anchor, string snugly touching the corner of her chin and tip of her nose, Honey coughed behind her hand.

"See? She did that every time I got to full draw. Every time. I only let down half of the time, so I didn't realize at the time. She said she had a cold, but with the crowds cheering, coaches, the wind, I guess I just…" She trailed off and stared at the screen.

My heart twisted in my chest for her. Her high-pitched voice was empty and tiny, like a child who lost her favorite toy. "When did you figure it out?" Even as I hurt for her, I wondered if it was motive for murder.

"Today. I've known I had an issue with letting down for a while. There was a world event a few years ago with such awful wind that we had to wear weighted backpacks to keep from tipping over. I let down a lot. It got to my head. I was working with my coach and a sport psych person. I'm pretty much over it now."

Mary nodded along with Owley, so she continued.

"Yesterday, Bruce pulled me aside to make sure I knew about the letting-down issue. He was very kind about it, but it bothered me 'cause I thought that no one else noticed. This morning, I decided to check the last time Bruce could've seen me shoot, and it became obvious."

"Hey guys, you about ready to head over to the Honey celebration thing?" Minx was walking over.

Tiger trotted past her and ruffled Owley's hair. "What's going on, kiddos?"

Owley looked at him and smiled briefly. "Honey was awful." She slammed shut her computer, got up, and wiped off her butt. "I'm gonna go put this in my room. Wait for me here."

Tiger and Minx sat down. Moo commando-crawled over to them. Tiger scratched behind Moo's ears. "Cool Batman shirt. Why is Honey awful? Besides the obvious, of course."

Mary looked at Tiger, and the words tumbled out of her mouth. "She just figured out that Honey had played mind games to win their match at the Summer Games. I'm not sure if she knew, but Honey somehow knew exactly what she needed to shoot to go against Owley."

Minx had been giving Moo a scratch behind the head. "That's what that was all about. She wanted to sandbag, of course. She gave us all phones and said we should each partner up and share the scores live. She was really insistent. So the guys watched us, and we watched them. I never really looked at the scores at the time. Did you know?" Minx had turned to look at Tiger.

"Oh that, yeah. Honey told me what the deal was later. She thought she was so smart, but the whole situation was kinda weak."

Minx rolled her eyes. "Don't act like you weren't Team Honey. Owley and I saw you two going at it like rabbits yesterday morning. We went to your room before the seminar started and saw you two through the window. Geez, you could at least close the blinds."

"You're just jealous." Tiger made kissy noises at Minx.

"Jealous? I'm gonna need therapy. Your big bare butt will haunt my nightmares."

This did not jive with what Tiger had said earlier. "You told me that you two weren't really a couple, that it was just for TV."

Tiger looked back at me. "That's true. She came over to talk about the TV stuff, and I suggested we had better practice being a couple. One thing led to another…"

Minx chuckled. "You're such a dog."

"You have wounded me, my lady. I'm a gentleman."

"Oh yeah, such a gentleman that the night before the Men's Team Event your teammates were going door to door looking for you. Who were you with?" Minx waggled her eyebrows at him.

Tiger looked down his nose at her. "A gentleman never kisses and tells. And I don't know why you're being such a pain in the butt. Are you still pissed about the Toxosports sponsorship?"

I jerked my head to Tiger. "Toxosports?"

Tiger poked Minx in the arm. "Didn't mention that, did you? Toxosports was looking at one of the US female archers to be the new face of the company. Minx was a shoo-in until Honey found out and scooped it out from underneath her."

Minx smacked him with the back of her hand. "It wasn't that big of a deal."

Tiger stuck a finger at her. "Tsk, tsk. You shouldn't lie. Honey told me all about it. It was a pretty sweet deal. She also told me that she had gotten the deal once she talked about her TV show and her ample charity work."

Minx crossed her arms over her chest. "By charity work, I assume you mean having sex with you, 'cause that's as close as she ever got to helping the unfortunate."

"She got a local soup kitchen to write a glowing letter about her after she made a sizable donation."

"So like everything in life, she bought it." Minx took an elastic band out of her pocket and pulled her hair back into a pony tail. "It's okay, there'll be other sponsors."

There would be a lot more sponsors for Minx with Honey dead. One thing was bothering me, and it had nothing to do with the case. Glaring at Tiger, I asked,

"How could you stand to be around Honey if you knew all this?"

He held up his hands defensively. "Hey, hey, I have enough troubles on the men's side of the field. I don't have time to borrow trouble from the ladies."

Minx shook her head. "You wouldn't know this, Princess, but Tiger has had a crush on Honey forever. She told me that she could always count on him to be there when she needed him. And when she didn't…" She reached out to pat him on the shoulder, but he shrugged her hand off.

"I like a pushy girl who knows what she wants, but it wasn't a crush. I'm not twelve."

"Mary. Di." Our names bounced around the large room as Jess yelled from the doorway. "Get over here right now."

We got up to join her. She grabbed my arm and marched up to my office, passing Owley in the hallway.

Jess hissed in my ear. "Door. Open it now."

I unlocked the door and stepped inside. "How can I help you, Jess?"

"What are you two doing? Bruce practically had a nervous breakdown in my office. We're already in the middle of a crisis, and you plan this Celebration of Life thing? Somehow I had to get liquor for it, 'cause Tiger said that we have to toast her. I had to do that after trying to assure Elizabeth that everything would be okay, but she ended up patting my back while I cried. I could just kill both of you. If you do one more thing to mess things up, I swear I will shoot you both out of a cannon. You got it?" Jess stared at us, chest heaving.

"Yes, ma'am," I said. Mary was gripping my arm for dear life and nodding.

Jess looked at us and let out a deep sigh. "I'm just… this has been a long day, and I don't want any more excitement. The police are mostly gone except a guy in his car out front. I told him that he could stay inside, but he said he should stay in the car. I walked by, and he was playing games on his phone. As soon as this thing is over tonight, I want you both to go to your room and not leave until I tell you to, got it?"

We nodded, and she stormed out of the room. I let out a breath I hadn't realized I was holding until then. "Wow, she's mad."

"Like Commissioner Gordon mad. We'll need to be sneakier. We have a few minutes; let's talk about what we know so far." Mary laid out the tablet and notebook, adding a few more notes.

"Sneakier? If we sneak at all, Jess will kill us."

Mary ignored me.

"I don't think this is a good idea anymore. It wasn't a great idea to begin with, but it isn't getting any better."

Mary snapped the lid on her pen and leaned back in her seat. "This is what we have so far. No one has a solid alibi. Jess is pissed that Honey died here so that is the opposite of a motive. Bruce was being blackmailed by Honey and thought she was going to ruin his career. Honey played head games with Owley at the Summer Games and took away her chance at a medal."

"But Owley said she didn't know until today," I pointed out.

"According to her. Someone is lying. Someone knows more than they are saying—unless you want to revisit the idea of the crazed stranger?" I shook my head; she was right. "Next up is Minx. She never liked Honey, and Honey took the Toxosports sponsorship. Minx could really use the money. Tiger had this thing with Honey; it's usually the lover. Then there's Liam——no motive, but he was in the building."

"He said he didn't do it, but that doesn't mean much. And you and I don't have any motive, right?" Mary looked at her notebook and shook her head no.

"Is there anything in the memoir that we haven't covered?"

"Nah." She pursed her lips and rolled her eyes over until they landed on me. "My money's on Owley. She's weird."

"You're so obsessed with weird. Then I'll take Bruce. He could have killed us in his office. My second choice is Minx. She's aggressive."

Mary snickered. "She reminds me of you. I'll take Tiger, even though he is far too cute to have killed her. And Jess, she was so mad that I really think she could have killed us."

"I guess that leaves Liam for me. You have Owley, Tiger, and Jess. I have Bruce, Minx, and Liam. Whoever is wrong has to clean the middle room of our unit for a month."

I got up. We were already late for the celebration of Honey's life.

Mary grabbed her tablet and notebook. "What about us? I'll take you and you take me?"

"If you killed Honey," I told her, "I'll take a new roommate."

CHAPTER SEVEN

We spent a few minutes going to the bathroom, checking our hair, and generally avoiding the Celebration of Life. I was the one who "planned" it, even if that was accidental. By the time we arrived, people were pretty tipsy. Empty beer cans lay on their sides like fallen soldiers. I had never enjoyed beer. There was a large pitcher of orange juice. I poured a glass and pulled a long sip before I realized that it was primarily vodka.

"Good gracious, no one light a match."

Mary took a sniff of her own glass then handed it to me and instead swiped a bottle of water off the table.

"You don't drink?"

She shrugged. "Sometimes. Maybe some wine with my family, but not much. I'm an easy puker."

"Good choice, then."

The room was mostly empty, with just the seven of us there. Owley and Tiger were at a table, quietly talking and drinking. Jess and Bruce shared another booth and were not even looking at each other while they took long drinks of their beers. Minx had a glass of the vodka with a hint of orange juice.

Minx waved her glass at us. "Glad you ladies could join the party you planned. You wanna get started so we can get back to drinking away this awful day?"

I looked around for Liam. I had thought he would be here. "Shouldn't we wait for Liam?"

Jess called over from her seat. "No, you just missed him. He said to start without him, but he'll be back soon."

I cleared my throat and didn't have a clue what to say. I hadn't planned a speech and wasn't sure if I could wing one. "Death is sad, and Honey's is no less so. We are sad."

That was awful. I looked around, and my eyes landed on Tiger. He had nice things to say about Honey. "Tiger, would you like to say a few words?"

Tiger looked at me, and I instantly regretted my choice. His eyes were glazed and unfocused. He set down his beer with the slow but jerky manner of a man losing control of his limbs. His tongue stuck out between his teeth as he carefully scooted out of the booth. It took an eternity. How drunk was he?

He looked around the room then grabbed the booth's back to steady himself. "Honey. Honey was… Honey was an awful person who deserved to die. Cheers, everyone." He reached for the drink he had set down but hit it with the back of his hand, knocking it over and spilling a small puddle of beer on the table. Owley giggled and wiped up the mess. Her giggles took on a life of their own, and she couldn't stop. Tiger started laughing too, and shortly they were howling with laughter, clutching their stomachs.

Everyone, not just me, was staring at them. "What's wrong with you?"

Minx got up and grabbed a bottle of water. Handing it to Tiger, she said, "Drink," then she turned to me. "Remember when he said he couldn't be bothered with drama from the women's side of the field? Well, the drama crossed the field."

Tiger downed the entire bottle, then his eyes got huge. He covered his mouth and stumbled from the room. Owley chased him out the door, asking if he was okay.

Minx shook her head and sat down. “He got an email from Honey’s agent after you guys left. Not a very good agent, since he didn’t know Honey was gone. I don’t think Tiger was supposed to be included, but it spelled out that Honey had said she was looking for a guy to replace Tiger if he wasn’t a big enough deal. She was trying to find a *real* athlete to replace him.” She put heavy emphasis on the word real.

Mary cringed. “Ouch.”

The faint sound of vomiting carried into the room from the hallway. Jess got up. “I guess I better check that he managed to hit a trashcan or something.”

The vodka was making my skin tingle. It was already making me feel lighter and clearer. I finished off my glass, and it was not nearly as sharp as my first taste. I grabbed the second glass, which appeared to have lost a few sips to a smiling Mary, who was sitting next to a smirking Minx.

“Minx, do you want to say anything?”

She got up and raised her glass. “To Honey. May she find all the things in the thereafter that she couldn’t find here.” She raised her glass, and those remaining in the room drank with her.

The vodka was making me feel loose and easy. Mary and I sat across from Minx and drank our respective drinks for a few minutes. The room was quiet but not tense. Everyone was lost in their own thoughts.

Minx eventually spoke up. "Mary, I meant to ask earlier. How's your mom doing these days?"

Before I even thought, my mouth was moving. "Why does everyone keep asking you that?" A thought flittered through my mind that I was slightly beyond tipsy.

"Oh, she had breast cancer, but she's fine now." She patted my hand.

Minx gasped at me. "Shut the front door, you didn't know that her mom had cancer? Aren't you guys roommates and, like, best buddies?"

I glared at her. She had been taking jabs at me since we met, and anger rose up in my chest like a snake.

Mary waved her hands. "Hey, no, it's no big deal. I never mentioned it and Di is private so—"

Minx glared right back and cut Mary off. "No, it is a big deal. Princess has been poking around all day into worse things in our lives but is too good to share anything about her life."

"Don't call me Princess."

"If the shoe fits, then you gotta lace it up and wear it, Princess. You think you're better than the rest of us." She tore her eyes off me to look at Mary. "Do you know anything about Princess? Does she have siblings? Why did she get divorced? Do you know anything about her?"

Mary stuttered but gave no answer.

Jess had returned with Tiger and cautiously came over. "Is everything okay over here?"

Minx turned around. "You guys are friends from way back. Do you know why Di got divorced and ran away from California? Honey said that's what happened."

"That is none of our business Minx. If Di wants to share the story, she will."

"No, no, she won't. That's the problem. She thinks she's too good to share anything."

The anger, shame, and vodka fought inside me. More than anything, I wanted to knock that smug look off Minx's face. "Fine!" My voice echoed in the large room. "If you want the story of why I'm divorced, then you'll get it."

Mary and Jess made quieting noises, but I was rolling, and nothing would stop me now. The stress of the past year, the drama of the past day, and my anger at Minx and her big mouth all came to a head at once. Emotions had been bottled up for too long, and they were spilling out everywhere. "It was my thirtieth birthday earlier this year, and my husband, Chris, had rented this party bus and invited a bunch of my friends to go out for drinks for girls' night, including my best friend, Beth." I put finger quotes around best.

"We were leaving the restaurant pretty well drunk when Chris calls to ask how things were going. I said we were just about to get to the comedy club and would be home later. After the call, I realized I left something at the house so the party bus stops at my house. Everyone wants to come in and say hi to Chris or use the bathroom, so we all go in through the garage, which opens into kitchen."

Minx interrupted me. "Are you hoping that we die of boredom before you have to tell us what happened?"

"Shut your face, Minx, I'm gonna tell this story the way I want to. Once we enter the kitchen, I see them."

Mary leaned forward as I pause for dramatic effect. "Who?"

"A man having sex with a gal leaning over the kitchen table. I just stand there. This couldn't be my house. Maybe we entered the wrong one. Maybe that is the Carlsons having sex. I look around and momentarily I don't recognize the room. Then everything snaps into focus. That's my husband and our interior decorator bent over the table. I don't recognize our kitchen because it has been so heavily remodeled this year. No wonder we had spent the past two years redoing the entire house."

Everyone was hanging on my every word. I felt powerful, finally getting it all out. I had carried the shame, and the more I hid it the heavier it got. But now that I was sharing it, it was light as a feather. I felt a freedom that intoxicated me far more than the vodka.

Jess shook her head. "Di, that is so awful."

I waggled a finger at her. "That's only half the story. To recap, I'm staring at Chris schtupping the interior decorator. I haven't moved an inch, but Beth has. My best friend, Beth, had pushed past me and grabbed him by his bits and pieces. She's hitting him with her purse while he's making this awful high-pitched screeching noise and trying to get away from her emasculating fist. Then I realized she's screaming at him."

I looked around to make sure everyone was

watching. "She's yelling, 'You said I was the only one' over and over."

Minx gasped. "Oh crap, happy birthday, Princess." She started giggling under her breath.

I couldn't help myself. I started giggling, too. At some point I had moved far enough away from the moment to see how ridiculous and awful it was. I had held so tight to the pain, never sharing it, that I wasn't able to see that I had started to heal.

Owley called out from where she was sitting next to Tiger, her arm intertwined with his. "Then what happened?"

"I left out one of the best parts of the story. Beth was drunker than a skunk, and she was hitting him so hard that eventually she lost her balance. The only thing she had a grip on was his gentleman's sausage. When she fell, I guess she yanked or smashed or twisted. I'm not totally clear on the details, but I guess he sprained it."

Mary gasped loudly and covered her mouth with her hands. "Men can sprain their winkies?"

I nodded. "Apparently. It was all a blur after that. The paramedics showed up and took him away. They were very professional and didn't laugh in his face while loading him onto a stretcher. Someone shuffled out the interior decorator. A couple of them grabbed a sobbing Beth before I could kill her. It was an even bigger betrayal than Chris."

Owley smiled and nodded her head in agreement, yelling out, "Dang skippy."

I took a moment to sit down across from Minx and next to Mary. Jess pulled out the remaining chair. Bruce turned back to his beer while Owley and Tiger leaned close and chatted.

Minx, Mary, and Jess looked at me, so I decided to finish out the story.

"Then Patsy, who got divorced the year before, sat me down and gave me the number to her lawyer and helped me figure out what to do next." I had shared so much that the rest just came rushing out. "That was what really killed me. When Patsy had gotten a divorce, I had told Chris that I pitied her. We had all seen it coming, and 'How could Patsy be so blind?'"

I took a napkin from the dispenser and patted my eyes. "I was so sure that I was smarter than her. Then one day, bam, my husband was banging half the neighborhood, and I had no idea."

Minx gave me a gentle smile. "I think that happens

to a lot of people, Princess. It doesn't mean you're stupid."

Maybe it was the cathartic release of getting everything off my chest, but I was no longer angry at her. "Now you like me, eh?"

Minx reached across the table and gave my hand a quick squeeze. "Actually, I just might."

Warmth settled around me as I sipped on my orange juice and vodka. The adrenaline of my fight with Minx left me feeling a bit shaky and tired but also free and clean. I let my mind wander over the details of the day when something clicked. I turned to Mary.

"The female archer who missed the Summer Games trials because her mother was sick in the hospital…"

Mary nodded her head. "Yeah, that was me."

I tried to be sensitive to the fact that she might not want to tell the story. "Do you want to talk about it?"

She shrugged her shoulders. "Sure. I think everyone else knows. My senior year in high school, my mom was diagnosed with breast cancer. I decided to skip college for a while to help her, plus I could train full-time. That's when I started doing the occasional archery article for extra money. You can compete in the youth division until the end of the year you turn twenty, so I did that. Her treatment was going great, and I never really thought she could die. The week of the trials, she was not feeling well, and I knew something was wrong, but I wanted to go 'cause it was the Summer Games. I was ranked second. The first day of the event, I got a phone call right in the middle of shooting. I answered, and Dad said she was in the hospital and they didn't think she was going to make it."

Her voice was clear, but tears made little rivers down her face. She wiped them off her chin, where they had collected.

"I don't remember much after that. Jess was there. She got my flight changed, packed me up, and took me to the airport. I sobbed the whole way home. I almost missed my connecting flight because the layover was short and I was way in back. I started calling out, 'Please let me out, my mom is dying, please let me get off, I'm gonna miss my flight.' People stepped back into the seats to let me out."

We had grabbed napkins to dab at our faces while she finished.

"I got to the hospital, and nothing else mattered but being there for my mom. I was so ashamed that I thought archery was more important. I held her hand all night, and in the morning she was actually a bit stronger. The nurses and doctors were amazing. Mom was there for a month, and I was there every day. You know, I haven't touched my bow since that day."

Minx gasped. "You haven't?"

Mary shook her head and stared at the table. "Nope. It's in my room, but I haven't unpacked it since the trials. Sometimes I open the bowcase to look at it, but it messes with my head. First I was super guilty 'cause I knew Mom was sick but I thought the trials were more important, which is so stupid. Nothing is more important than family. Then it got to a point where I'm not even sure I can shoot anymore. Maybe I've lost whatever I had."

Jess shook her head. "That's not how it works. Shooting archery isn't some magical spark that you can lose. Whenever you are ready, we can get you back to the level you were at. But no rush."

If she wasn't shooting, then…? "How did you end up here?"

"Mom eventually got better, and now she's in remission. It was the right time for me to go to college, but I felt out of synch with everyone else. Remember when I said that Elizabeth is a hero of mine?"

I nodded my head.

"I used to have a Westmound Sponsorship. It is like the best one in the industry. When I left the trials, she called me right away. She said I did the right thing leaving, and they would be praying. After that, she checked on me every month or so. She never pressured me to get back to competing but did say that whenever I was ready, she would like to help. I heard about the center here and that Jess and Robbie were slated to work here. I called Elizabeth and asked about living here. It just seemed right. Archery has been my second family my entire life, and it would be like being with family while I attended the state college."

I pursed my lips. "You could have told me all this, you know."

She shrugged her shoulders. "When you came and didn't want to talk about anything personal, I thought that was awesome. I didn't have to talk either. I could just pretend nothing had happened."

Minx snorted. "Birds of an emotionally unhealthy feather flock together, eh?"

I giggled. "Mary, I think we both need therapy. I'll go if you go." I threw my arms around her and stole a quick hug. "If you are this hot-shot archer, then why don't you go by a pro name like everyone else?"

"I kinda do. Mary is my real name but they call me Bloody Mary 'cause I can really destroy a bracket. Even if I qualify low, it is almost guaranteed that I will knock out the higher-ranked archers. Something about the head-to-head competition really ups my game."

"Wow, intimidating."

Mary, Minx, Jess, and I sniffled and laughed, when a voice broke through. "Why is Moo wearing a Batman shirt?"

I looked up to see Liam had joined us. "It's hard to explain."

Jess got up. "I'm going to check on Tiger." Minx followed along behind, carefully balancing a bowl of tiny pickles, a second bowl of olives, beer, a plastic glass of OJ and vodka, and a potato chip bag clenched between her teeth.

Liam pulled out the chair opposite me and sat down. Moo got up from where he was lying and shoved his head between the table and Liam's chest. "Hey buddy, have you done a good job of keeping Di and Mary out of trouble?" He cast a meaningful look at me.

I hitched my chin up in what I hoped was a

delightfully defiant look. He looked even more handsome tonight; maybe I have a thing for Vikings. His hair looked so soft, I wondered how it felt. I quickly shook my head to clear my mind. "You're not my boss; you can't tell me what to do."

Mary poked me in the arm. "Um, he kinda is."

How the heck is the equipment guy kind of my boss? "I was just kidding. We've been staying out of trouble."

With one eyebrow raised, he didn't seem to believe me. "You haven't been Nancy Drew-ing around, trying to solve the mystery?"

"More like Caped Crusading, but if I was, then I would have asked about your motive." I was pleased with how smoothly I had worked that in.

"And I would have told you that I have no motive. I didn't really know her all that well. She applied for a sponsorship through Westmound, which I'm in charge of, but we turned her down. But the real clincher is that I have an airtight alibi."

I looked at Moo, who was meticulously scratching his huge ears with his back paw, looking very much like a huge bat. "I'm not sure if Moo would be allowed to testify in court."

Liam chuckled deeply. "Moo would say anything for some f-o-o-d. But I was actually referring to the video surveillance."

"The center doesn't have surveillance cameras." It was on a to-do list in my office.

"The center doesn't, but the equipment room does. We have one of everything made by Westmound or Westmound-owned companies, plus accessories, tools, and"—he leaned in close—"we might have a few products from competitors."

"Who's on it?"

He leaned back in his seat. "I don't know who's on it, and I'm not sure if you can even see the door. We had it installed when the center was built. It's set into a bullet-proof box in the far corner of the room. It took all day to get the police the footage. The guy who installed it had to drive over from headquarters with the key and walk the police through the process of getting the card, or downloading or whatever. They left not too long ago, then I went to clean up the mess in there."

Mary and I exchanged a meaningful glance when Liam looked at Moo then darted out of his seat.

"Can you stay here for a bit? I need to grab something from my room. I just realized someone didn't get *dinner*." He mouthed the word dinner, and when we nodded, he jogged from the room.

As soon as Liam disappeared into the hallway, Mary grabbed my arm and squealed. "Quick, we have ten minutes tops. Let's go."

I had been too busy watching Liam's strong back and the way his jeans clung to him as he left and was slow to follow her train of thought. "Huh?"

"We have to go check out the equipment room. There is a window in the door. If we can see the camera, then we know that the police have footage of the killer. Come on." She was already out of her seat, grabbing my hands to pull me up. "Batdog, away."

The equipment room was just down the hallway and around the corner. We could easily get there, poke around for a minute or two, and be back before anyone even noticed. Moo and I followed her out the door and down the hallways when she suddenly stopped. "Dang it, I left my tablet and notebook. I'll go get them and be thirty seconds behind you."

Moo and I went around the corner and approached the door. The room was dark inside, and I squinted, hoping to catch sight of the camera. I tested the door handle; it was locked, but the latch hadn't caught. I opened the door and flipped the switch. The large room had cabinets, counters, and shelves running the perimeter of the entire room, with a huge table in the middle. The door was set by one corner of the room, while in the opposite corner, set into the wall, was a clear window. I scurried over to get a closer look. The corner did not have cabinets or shelves. I could faintly see something behind the clear panel. I was trying to figure out where the camera was pointing when I heard something behind me.

I turned around, expecting Mary, but instead Owley stood in the doorway, playing with a hammer. A cold prickle danced across my skin. "Hey, Owley, what are you doing here?"

Owley's face was split in two by a huge smile, much larger than natural. She stared at me while weaving slightly in the doorway. She giggled and tried to spin the hammer in her hand with thick, clumsy fingers. Moo pushed up against me, and the hairs on his neck lifted under my fingers.

"Owley are you okay?" I had seen her drink quite a bit tonight; maybe she was just drunk?

"I'm fine." Her words were slow, thick, and she almost sang them. "I took quite a few anti-anxiety pills, and I don't feel anxious anymore."

A low rumble that I felt from Moo more than heard echoed my feeling of discomfort. "I don't think you are supposed to mix those with alcohol."

Owley snarled at me and screamed, "Don't tell me what to do!" She threw the hammer over the table in my direction. I ducked and wrapped my body around Moo. The hammer banged off the table and hit the cabinet a foot to my right. "No one tells me what to do anymore, but you know that. You know!"

The area under the large table was filled with boxes, but I could see through a small space. Owley was still opposite me. "I don't know anything, Owley."

Another hammer flew through the air, this time hitting the shelves above the counter to my left. A waterfall of tiny boxes hit the counter and floor, scattering ammo and tools everywhere. Moo barked.

"Don't act stupid. You know! You recognized my shoes." A hammer hit a shelf about eight feet to my right this time. A horrible crash rained down complicated equipment I didn't recognize.

"Why are there so many hammers in here?" So far nothing had hit me or Moo. I kept an eye on Owley's legs to make sure she didn't try to move around the table for a clearer shot at us.

"They're your shoes. I took them after you dropped them by Honey's body. Minx said to make Honey respect me, and boy did I show her. No one will disrespect me again."

Finally I was getting the information we had spent all day searching for, and I couldn't focus. Where was Mary? If Moo got hurt, I would be destroyed. I thought of him as my dog, even if he was with me only part time. He was part of my new family, my new home, the new life I was building here. I could catch glimpses of Owley from under the table. She was playing with a big rubber mallet, bouncing it off the countertop.

She stopped suddenly. "I was so happy when you told that story. I knew you meant it for me. You caught your husband cheating and wanted to kill the girl. I caught Tiger cheating, and I did kill the girl. I'm even better than you."

I was sniveling on the floor, wiping my tears on Moo's shirt, when the mallet banged on the cabinet above my head. It bounced off hard and hit me in the temple. I saw a flash of light and heard a bang. I was clutching my head when I realized the noise was not from my head but the doorway. Peeking under the table,

I saw more legs than before.

Liam's strong voice broke through the chaos. "Get the officer; he's in his car in front of the center. Run!"

A sob broke through my clenched throat. Peeping over the table, I saw Mary coming through the door while Liam had Owley with her arms behind her in the hallway.

I stood up and rushed quietly through the wreckage to hug Mary. "You guys came to save me. Where'd you go?"

Mary hugged me. "I'm so sorry. I went to get the notebook and tablet, but it was gone. Owley said Jess took it to her place. I went outside then ran into Liam. I explained, and he took off running, then we got here and…" She squeezed me around the neck. "I'm a lousy sidekick."

I hugged her back hard and lifted her off the ground. "You're the best sidekick ever."

We walked into the hallways, where Owley had lost whatever control she had left. She was talking to Liam, begging him to just let her go. "No, really, it's fine. Just let me go, and we can all pretend it never happened. No one even liked Honey."

Tiger turned the corner. "Minx just went running

down the hall. Is everything okay?" He saw Liam holding Owley and slowed. "What's going on?"

Owley brightened. "Tiger, tell them to let me go. Tell them it's okay that Honey is dead."

Tiger stopped and stared at her. "What did you do?"

"I knew that she was forcing you to pretend to be her boyfriend and have sex. Minx told me to make Honey show me respect, so when I saw her go to the center, I followed her to the weight room and told her to leave you alone. She just laughed at me and turned away. I grabbed that weight and just smacked her. It felt amazing. She fell down and never moved again."

Tiger's Adam's apple bounced on his neck. "Oh, Owley." His voice was heavy with his realization and disappointment.

"No, no, no, it's okay. She never felt a thing, and I'm fine. I did get blood all over my shoes. There was no way to clean them, then Di left me a pair in the weight room. I was able to get back to my room before anyone saw me. I ran out the back door. It's okay."

She was begging him to understand, but he stood there shaking his head. An officer ran around the corner, his eyes darting around the group.

Owley was blind to him. "I had to kill her, for us."

The officer moved over to Owley. I ran a hand over my face. My temple was throbbing (which I deserved for investigating alone). A pattering of voices was around me, but it had been such a long day, and so much had happened. A strong grip on my arm broke my thoughts.

"I recognize that look. Come over here and sit down." Liam directed me over to a wall to sit next to Moo.

I smiled gratefully at him. "I swear I'm not always like this. I normally go just days and days without nearly fainting."

"I'll believe it when I see it." He left me while Mary sat next to me up against the wall.

Mary leaned over and let her head fall on my shoulder. "Owley is out of her mind. Does that mean that the Joker did it?"

"Not even the Jack Nicholson version." I looked at Owley screaming at the officers. "Definitely the Heath Ledger version."

Minx had joined the group at some point and came over to sit on the floor opposite us. "Wow, so Owley killed Honey? I totally thought it was Di."

"Me? Why would you think I killed Honey?"

"You found her body, and you have this evil glint in your eye. That's why none of us wanted to be alone with you. We always made sure Mary was around, too."

Mary and I exchanged a surprised look. I hadn't considered it from that angle. "Did you know that Owley is saying that you told her to do this?"

Minx reeled back. "She what?"

I nodded my head then put on a falsetto to repeat what Owley had screamed at me. "Minx said to make Honey respect me, and boy, did I show her. No one will disrespect me again."

Minx shook her head. "Wow, that is not how I meant it at all."

We all sat in silence and watched Owley. She was ranting at the officers, in turn pleading then yelling then crying. Several more had joined the first officer, and a few more appeared around the corner. It was like last night all over again.

Mary asked, "Do you think she just snapped?"

Minx turned back toward us. "Yeah, Honey had walked all over her for years, and Owley hated her, but I didn't realize it went so deep."

Minx had joined us late and missed the interaction

between Owley and Tiger. "I think Tiger was the final straw."

Minx's eyebrows knit together. "Tiger?"

Upon hearing his name, Tiger looked around. He spotted us and collapsed on the floor next to Minx. "I can't believe she killed Honey. We weren't even that serious."

Minx fiddled with her fingernails. "You and Honey weren't that serious?"

"No, Owley and I weren't."

"Are you serious, Tiger? I could've told you that was a bad idea. Is she who you were with at the Summer Games?" Minx shook her head.

"I just needed to blow off some steam. We've kept in touch since then but I didn't think it was serious."

Minx snorted. "Men."

Liam came over to sit next to me. "They have a search warrant. They would have found Owley even without someone's help." He gave me a meaningful look while I tried to avoid his eyes.

Jess rounded the corner and descended on our group. "What is going on? Why is everyone here? What did you do?"

The last question was directed at me. "What did I

do? I got hammers thrown at me for no good reason."

Mary pointed to the door. "I can't believe she threw hammers. There are actually guns and bows in that room."

Liam shook his head. "I just cleaned it."

Jess looked at us huddled on the floor then at the police gathered around Owley. "Oh no, our women's recurve program has taken a serious blow. In one day we lost two of our top three ranked archers. Who's gonna fill the gap?"

I looked at Mary. We exchanged a side hug and burst out laughing.

ABOUT THE AUTHOR

Nikki Haverstock lives with her husband and dogs on a cattle ranch high in the Rocky Mountains.

Before escaping the city, Nikki taught collegiate archery for ten years. She has competed on and off for fifteen in the USA Archery women's recurve division.

Nikki has more college degrees than she has sense, and hopefully one day she will put one to work.

Learn more at http://NikkiHaverstock.com